THE GUNSLINGER BOLEJACK
A BAD MAN IS HARD TO BURY

L. GLEN ENLOE

For information contact: info@outlawspublishing.com
Cover Design by Outlaws Publishing
Published by Outlaws Publishing
May 2025
10987654321

Chapter 1

He sat atop his blood-red horse on the far edge of the sprawling 4,000-acre spread known as the Black Cross Ranch. A fading orange, yellow and maroon sunset silhouetted him like an icon on a church's stained-glass window.

"Now who is that?" asked the bent-over cowhand as he spat a wad of tobacco into the lush grass.

"Whoever he is, he shouldn't be here," the man next to him said. They both jerked their horses forward as they squinted into the last rays of the sun. "Clay don't like no trespassers on his land."

But as they galloped forward, the shadowed man seemed to vanish. They looked up and down the hill's edge as the colors faded but they could see nothing.

"Now where'd he go to?" Josh Barnes asked as they moved on. "He was just here!"

The two hired hands slowed their horses and finally stopped. They sat a moment in silence.

"You fellas looking for me?"

"But we…" then Josh stopped as he spat out another load of thick brown juice.

Gil Klammer, the man next to Josh began to draw his gun, but stopped. The business end of a Colt .45 was already leveled at him.

"Na… now we didn't mean no harm…" Josh stuttered as his large eyes got larger than ever. "We were just curious—as to who you was and what you're doing on Black Cross land…."

"Black Cross land?" the stranger said as he continued to level his gun at them.

"Why sure," Gil offered, "I reckon you didn't know you're on the Black Cross Ranch now."

"No, I didn't," the dark bronze-haired man said, "and I don't care."

"Don't care?" Josh blurted out, surprised.

"You're trespassing as we see it," Gil said coldly as his courage returned. "And if you didn't have that gun on us, we'd be ordering you off this land!"

"Ordering me off this land?" the stranger repeated. A big smile broke out on his handsome, clean-shaven face as he slid his Colt back into its holster.

"Why didn't you say so?" he continued as he trotted his dark crimson-colored horse up to the two men. He then held out his big paw like he wanted to a shake. "Guess I had you two all wrong," the man continued. "But I would have sworn this was Westrum land."

"Westrum land?" Josh stammered. He hadn't heard that name in years. He shook his head. "You're wrong. But no hard feelings." He reached for the strange man's offered hand.

In one swift hard motion the stranger seized Josh's hand in a powerful claw-like grip and then jerked the cowboy out of his saddle and onto the ground.

"What the…!?" Gil roared as he started to clear leather. But he was too slow as the man's big Colt flashed in the air and crashed with a sick thud against the side of his head. Gil fell off his horse like a stone as Josh managed to rise to his feet with his gun in hand. A quick blur of the stranger's size fourteen boot into Josh's jaw sent him flying backward and unconscious into the tall dry grass of the hillside. Then the stranger was gone.

Gil staggered to his feet, holding his ringing head. "Who the hell are you!?" he managed to scream into the evening wind. A dim voice seemed to echo back in the darkening sky, and then died.

Gil shook his head, trying to clear it. The boss wasn't going to like this. Not on his land. And he sure wouldn't cotton to anyone asking questions. He looked down at his still unconscious partner.

"Damn!" he said as he looked for his gun. "How could one man…."

Josh began to moan and then sat up. "Who was that train we run into?"

Gil Klammer squinted into the darkening evening sky. "Danged if I know… but I swear he yelled back something that sounded like 'Bolejack' when I yelled that same question."

Chapter 2

"So, this is Black Cross land now," the stranger said to himself as he wound down the narrow trail. It was full night now, and a chill had begun to settle over the darkening terrain. It had been so long ago. So long. As he recalled, there was a grubby upstart of a town a few miles ahead. *'What was its name? Did it even have a name? Morganville? Mayorwood?'* He couldn't quite recall.

A dim jaundiced light soon appeared up ahead. "It must be the town," he said to himself. He strained to read a sign up ahead by the dim light of a half-moon and twinkling cold white stars. "Maggotwood. Maggotwood? Now why would anyone name a town that?"

As he rode on, the dim yellow lights grew larger. Then the rotting false-fronts of bedraggled gray buildings came into view as a few scurrying ferret-like town residents seemed to scamper for cover, their bulging eyes flashing like white stones in a deep dark river.

The lonesome tinny plinking of an out-of-tune piano heralded what appeared to be the only saloon in town. An obligatory drunk stumbled through its gaudy batwings as Bolejack stepped down from his horse and carefully tied its reins to a broken hitching rail.

The low undertone of glasses clinking, people talking and saloon girls laughing suddenly ceased as Bolejack pushed open the creaking swinging doors. Only the discordant piano pounding continued for a few seconds before the music man's hands froze and the lit cigar between his yellow clinched teeth fell to the floor.

The man called Bolejack stood there for a moment savoring the silence that his muscular 6-foot 5-inch frame always had on people when he encountered them for the first time. Then he pushed on through the doorway. The saloon noise started up again.

"What you want stranger?" The big pot-bellied barkeep growled as Bolejack stopped in front of the long mahogany bar.

"Westrum," Bolejack said, his voice steady as he looked the man in his eye for a reaction.

"Westrum? I never heard of that kind of whiskey," the saloon man said dully. "We got Overholt and a few others…."

"You're not as dumb as you talk," Bolejack observed quietly as a smile briefly fluttered across his lips. "I'll have a beer."

"Sure."

Three cowpokes to his left at the far end of the bar had suddenly perked up. They eyed him darkly as he watched them in the back mirror. The biggest of the three, nearly as tall as Bolejack, slowly inched his way closer. As he neared, Bolejack noticed two other cowboys tense up at a table behind him as the other patrons of the bar began to move away.

"Did I hear you mention the name 'Westrum'?" the big puncher asked.

"I did," Bolejack replied as his hand gripped his beer tightly. "What of it?"

The large cowpoke paused, as if startled by the response. Then he composed himself. "Folks don't talk about Westrum in this town or on Black Cross land."

"I do," the stranger answered as he took a long sip of his slightly warm beer and pretended to ignore the puncher. He slowly finished the beer and then turned to the man with the glass still in his large hand. "It could have been colder."

"Colder? What?"

"The beer. And by the way, how do you know Westrum?"

The cowboy's big blocky face began to turn red as his two partners at the bar sauntered up behind him. "Me?!" he muttered. "I should be asking you that!"

"And who are you?" Bolejack innocently asked with a smile.

"Me? Why I'm the foreman of the Black Cross! That's who I am!"

"Name?"

"Name? Damn it, I'm Chick Swickard and…"

But the shattering of the beer mug into Chick's forehead stopped his words. His two friends had their guns out within three seconds, but that wasn't fast enough. Two short blasts from Bolejack's Colt silenced them for eternity as they fell on top of the writhing bloodied foreman known by his poultry nickname.

Bolejack then swung his smoking gun toward the other two onlookers who had knocked over their table and had started to reach for their guns.

"I wouldn't!" Bolejack said, his deep voice rising. "If you want to live—"

He slowly backed out of the now nearly empty saloon with his guns leveled on the men. "You too!" he admonished the fat barkeep who had started to reach under the bar. "Your guts wouldn't look nice on that shiny new back mirror…."

Then he was through the swinging doors and on his horse. As he turned to ride away, he noticed the name of the bar for the first time: Dead Carcass Saloon. They got that right, he said to himself as he spurred his horse. Dead right.

Chapter 3

Isac Augustus Karp stood over the two dead Black Cross cowboys as Chick Swickard rubbed his bandaged head. Karp then nervously fingered the dull gold watchchain that was draped across his vest.

"They're dead," Karp proclaimed like it was a revelation of the greatest importance. Isac Karp, the mayor, coroner, undertaker and main driving force behind Maggotwood, straightened his ponderous suited bulk and idly combed back the last few remaining long strands of greasy red hair he had over his shining pate. Strangely jolly for a man of his varied occupations, Karp emptied the pockets of the two deceased men and counted his landfall.

"They just got paid yesterday," Chick offered.

Karp stroked the lower of his double chins and pondered. "Well, at least they didn't drink it all up," he sighed. "There's enough for their funerals, but not much else." Within his mind he was contemplating the viability of squeezing the two skinny cowhands into one pine box to save money. Maybe.

There had been no sheriff, marshal or any other form of law to come rushing into the Dead Carcass Saloon after the shooting. None existed. Maggotwood couldn't afford any law. In fact, they couldn't afford much of anything. In truth, the sway-backed little town fully lived up to its unofficial cynical moniker of 'the town too dead to live.'

But that didn't bother Isac Karp. He liked it that way. It was his town, no matter how loathsome, vile and despicable it was. It was all his. The only other competition in the territory was Clay Black. But they had long had an unwritten and unspoken understanding. Karp had Maggotwood, and Black had the surrounding Black Cross Ranch. Between the two of them, they owned the world—at least the world as they knew it.

"That stranger was asking about Westrum," Chick said as he tried to get up from the barroom floor.

"Yeah, he sure did," the burly barkeep joined in, "just out of the blue."

"Westrum? King Westrum?" Karp echoed as he leaned against the bar. "Now that's a name I haven't heard for a while—at least not since the raids."

"And that's the way Clay likes it," Chick said as he drew himself up to the blood-spattered bar. "He's going to go bug-eyed when he hears somebody's asking around about him again."

Karp brushed aside a few errant blood spots with his sleeve as he picked up a glass of whiskey. "How about cleaning this mess up, Pock?" he said.

Pock Johnson, so-called by the numerous small pox scars on his puffy face, grunted and picked up his towel. "Sure boss."

"Don't call me that," Karp admonished him, wanting to keep his ownership of the bar as discreet as possible although everyone in town had already guessed it.

"Swamper already mopped up in front," Johnson said, "guess he forgot the bar top."

Karp grunted and then belched. "Chick, you and the boys can haul them on over to my office," he said, waving his sausage-like fingers in the air at the corpses. "You can tell Black."

Chick flushed as he grabbed an arm of one of the dead men. "Guess there's no way around it."

"Be sure to tell him about Westrum's name being mentioned. And tell him we need to talk."

"Sure Karp." As they dragged the two dead cowhands away, Isac Karp reflected on the stranger who had shot up the saloon. Westrum. Who would be asking about King Westrum after all these years?

Chapter 4

"So, you let this stranger come riding in on my land big as you please, and then he knocks you two silly before you can draw your guns?" Clayton Black ran his fingers quickly through his steel-gray streaked black hair as his face reddened. "What am I paying you boys for?!" he erupted as he turned his back on them in disgust.

"But boss…" Josh Barnes stammered. "He caught us off-guard."

"That's right," Gil joined in, "and then, all sudden like, he holsters his gun and wants to shake our hands!"

"You fools—" Clay Black said under his breath.

"But…"

"Get back to work before I fire you both! If I weren't so short-handed as it is, I'd…"

"Sure boss, sure," Josh said as the two turned away.

But Gil stopped and turned back. "We almost forgot…"

"Forgot what? Your brains?" Clay almost shouted. "Did that stranger knock them out, too?"

"He was asking about… Westrum."

The rage in Clay Black's face suddenly died. "Westrum?" His florid face dimmed and grew strangely pale.

"Yes, sir."

"Get out!"

Josh and Gil slunk out the front door of Black's large sprawling ranch house not looking back.

"Westrum," Black repeated as he half-stumbled to his huge leather and horn chair next to his ornate desk. He settled back in the over-sized chair and sighed softly. For him, this monstrosity of a throne had become a symbol of his importance and dominance of the region. He was king here now. Not Westrum. Not anymore. Black bowed his head in deep thought. Suddenly, he felt old. Very old.

******

The next day Clayton Black was back to his old self. And why shouldn't he be, he told himself as he watched the crew saddling up their horses to ride out for the day. But something didn't seem right. Then he realized what it was. Five of his men were missing. "!"Damn, he scolded himself, he knew he shouldn't have allowed some of them to ride into town the previous day. They'd probably gotten drunk and wound up in what passed for the jail in Maggotwood: Isac Karp's backroom morgue. It had happened before. Along with being coroner and his other duties, the self-proclaimed straw boss of town did what little marshaling that went on there, too.

They'll be riding in soon, he told himself as he watched his daughter Rosemarie help clean up the morning dishes. She didn't really need to, that was the hired man's job, but she enjoyed helping. At times she even helped with some of the cooking, much to the dismay of their Chinese cook. But after a while, when he realized his wages wouldn't suffer from the help, Leng Po just smiled and nodded, glad for the help.

It was almost noon and still the missing five ranch hands had not shown up. Black, a man of medium height and weight, furrowed his brow as he stared into the hills. He was most of all concerned about his foreman not being there. It wasn't like Chick to do something like this. He had always been the one with the level head.

Now nearing sixty-six years of age, Clay Black was at the peak of his power and wealth. His ranch had been wildly successful over the years, but on the near horizon he could feel that things and times were changing. The weather had become as unpredictable as ever, and the cattle business had finally began slacking off the last few years. The great cattle drives were now becoming a thing of the past. At his age, he had to think ahead about the future. Was it nearing time to sell out? But what then? This was all he knew. And soon he knew his daughter and only heir would mostly likely be leaving. She's already had marriage proposals, but had turned them down. With her mother dead from the fever ten years ago, he was the only thing that was holding her here.

Then he saw them, three riders loping back up the trail over the hills from town. But only three? There should be two more.

He stood out on the large winding porch that curved around the front of the ranch house and watched. His daughter joined him.

Chick Swickard slowly dismounted and tied his buckskin horse to the rail as the other two cowhands followed suit.

"Sorry we're late," Chick said shamefacedly. He glanced back at the other two.

"There should be two more of you. Where's the other two?" Clay asked, afraid of what he'd hear. He could smell whiskey on Chick's breath even several feet away.

"Dead," Chick said matter-of-factly. "Some stranger shot them at the saloon last night."

"Looks like you had a hand in it," Black observed as he eyed Chick's bandaged and bloodied head.

"He slammed a glass into me and then shot Floyd and Arlan before we could hardly blink."

The dark redness had returned to Black's face. "And you other two were just too slow to pull down on his mystery man? Is that it?"

They nodded and looked away, not saying a word. They had spent most of the morning drinking to bolster their courage. It hadn't worked.

"Damn, first Josh and Gil, and now you boys." Black ran his hand through his hair as he often did when he was at a loss for words. "I thought I'd hired some hands that could both work and fight!" he snorted. "Guess I was wrong!"

Chick gathered up his courage as Black turned away. "Westrum!" he blurted out suddenly. "That big stranger was talking about Westrum."

Clay stopped in his tracks, turned and took a few steps toward Chick.

"Westrum!" Black pulled back his hand and struck Chick across the side of his face sending he backwards.

"Father!?" Rose yelled as she went to Chick's aid. But he was already up and backing away.

"Don't ever say that name to me again," Black said as the three cowhands retreated to their horses. "Get out of here and get to work! You've already lost half a day!"

"Dad…" Rose said sadly as she stood there watching the three gloomily ride away. "That's not like you…."

"Maybe it is or it isn't," Clay said as he turned away and disappeared into the house.

Rosemarie stood there on the porch for a few minutes trying to comprehend what she'd witnessed. She had never seen her father so out of control. *'And who,'* she wondered, *'was this Westrum?'*

Chapter 5

They had opened a new cemetery closer to town since Bolejack had been there. He lingered a moment at its entrance and then shook his reins. There would likely be no one there that he knew. At least, none that he cared about. He headed on north.

About a half mile away he came upon a grown-up field of brush and small trees. He wasn't sure this was it, but it had to be. At its edge was a massive tree that legend said had once been the hanging place of several local outlaws. Straining, he squinted his eyes and finally made out the top of the largest tombstone. He dismounted and carefully made his way through the tall weeds and twisted brush. It was apparent that no one had kept the small graveyard maintained. Careful to keep an eye out for snakes, he walked toward the center of the old bone yard. He stumbled briefly over a fallen grave stone, but quickly regained his balance.

"Buhman. James W. Buhman…" he said aloud as he eyed the grave he had nearly fallen over. I think I remember that name, he said to himself. He was the owner of Maggotwood's first mercantile he recalled. He used to give him and his brother penny candy when his folks came in for supplies.

There were about twenty graves here now he estimated. Some had likely been moved to the new boot hill. He walked on. There they were.

The stones were over-grown with weeds. Even the writing seemed faded and dim: Robert James Westrum.

"Bobby…" Bolejack whispered. His brother. He had been three years older than Bolejack, and they had been almost inseparable. But now, even the image of his face was faded in Bolejack's mind.

And there, right next to Bobby, was his mother's slightly larger marker: Pearl Mae Westrum. She had been a kind, loving woman who had done her best to temper the stern nature of her husband. She had always put her own needs aside for her sons. Her lily-white face seemed to materialize right before Bolejack's eyes. *'Mama…'* a far away voice in his head seemed to whisper. *'Mama.'*

There was a strange moistness in his eyes that he rarely felt. He shook his head. There, looming to the right was the largest of the three tombstones. Westrum: Wallace King Westrum. Bolejack turned away. His father had been a good man, but a distant man. A private man. It seemed that no one really knew what his father was thinking at any given time. He was also a powerful man in his day. Even as just a child, he and his family had felt it. Yes, in those few short years his father had taught him most of what he would ever need to know about being a man. But had it been enough?

Then came the day that had changed everything. Only a sudden bellyache from eating too many green apples and a long session in the outhouse had saved him. Even his brother had scoffed at his foolishness before leaving him there in his sickness. But after hearing the shouting, the commotion and the shooting, he was still too sick and fearful to leave the privy. Finally, he got up and looked out the half-moon in the outhouse door as his mother and brother screamed. He stared helplessly as two dark horsemen dragged them through the yard. The strange men then roped his father and galloped their horses around dragging his thrashing body behind. Then there was a strange silence, and he could hear muted voices.

Where was he? One of the men asked. "Where was Billy—where was Billy?" the strange men screamed? Then they began looking for him as they dragged his family away. Only his father had quit screaming.

He remembered the sheer panic as they came near the outhouse. He recoiled from the half-moon and fell back on the crude bench. There was nothing else to do. He could feel his sickness returning. He lifted up the cover of the larger of the two holes and squirmed his way down into it feet first. He had to lift his arms up to pass through as he pulled the cover over him. He began throwing up again from the stench as he sank into the disgusting muck and liquid. Luckily, it was only a foot deep. Then he jammed his hands over his mouth and nose. He could hear the door of the outhouse open. "Not here," he heard one of them say as he continued to hold his breath. The door slammed shut. They were gone.

The old memory of the smell curdled his stomach as he remembered his humiliation. But he had survived. When quietness returned to the ranch, and he crawled from the primal ooze of the privy, he ran silently away to some nearby trees and a creek. The men were gone. He jumped into the water to clean himself, erase the images that tore at his tender belly.

It was only later that he learned the fate of his parents and brother: he'd heard some men on the road talking. They'd said his family had been dragged all around until they were just bloody masses. But he had not wanted to find out for himself and look that night. He still felt sick to his stomach and just wanted to get away. After rising from the water of the creek he had ran blindly. He ran for mile after mile, never looking back. That's when he had left the area, and had never came back. Till now.

A family of travelers by the name of Bolejack, on their way to California from Missouri, had found him walking along on the road a couple of days later. They already had three kids of their own and figured one more wouldn't make much difference. That's how he had wound up in the golden state. He had told them Indians killed his family and they seemed to believe him. Unfortunately, the law in California wasn't so believing, and a few years later said he couldn't stay with the Bolejacks. Then he was placed in an orphanage for several years. But that dark time was behind him. Now he was free, and he had returned—and only some sort of justice or retribution could satisfy him and truly make him free.

Bolejack's knees creaked loudly as he stood up. He wasn't sure why he clung to the name Bolejack. He was a Westrum. William Westrum. But he was also a Bolejack. He had become a man as a Bolejack. A real man. Yet a man in a child's body. He looked around. It would soon be dark. He had been at this forgotten boot hill longer than he intended. He looked at the three lonely grave stones again. He pulled off a gnarled wild grape vine that had wound around the base of King Westrum's marker. Yes, he was really Bill Westrum, not Bill Bolejack as everyone now knew him. But how could he be part of something he could only vaguely recall? He was Bolejack, simply Bolejack, and that was who he would always be—there was no turning back.

Chapter 6

Clay Black didn't like being seen going into the Dead Carcass Saloon. In fact, he didn't really like being associated with the likes of Isac Karp at all. There had been rumors about Karp and his wife years ago. Dark dirty rumors. He had tried to put it from his mind, but still it was there and quietly festering. But here he was. He hated to admit it to himself, but he still needed Karp.

"Isac here?' he asked the lethargic Pock Johnson as he pretended to wipe the bar. Pock was a short, but burly man with a slight hunchback. His scarred yet strangely puffy fact contorted in the dim ivory light of the saloon as he mulled over his answer.

"Sure, he's in the back," he finally said in a raspy voice. "He's been waiting for you."

Clay motioned to Chick Swickard, who had lingered on the threshold of the greasy bat-winged door, to come in. The two men then walked slowly past the empty faro tables and entered a seedy back room whose centerpiece was an ornate billiard table that had reportedly come all the way from St. Louis. Or so the story went. It took up nearly a quarter of room along with an equally ornate roll-top desk to one side. Isac Karp stood at the far end of the sporting table with cue in hand.

"Game over," Karp said flatly as he waved off a wiry bantam rooster of a cowpoke who quickly laid down his stick and left the room.

"Heard you wanted to see me," Clay offered, trying to mask his dislike of Karp.

"We have a mutual interest," the lord of Maggotwood began. "A stranger."

"Some of my boys have seen him. They say his name is Bolejack."

"Bolejack?!" Karp said, his face growing troubled. "I've never heard of any Bolejacks around here."

"Neither have I. But he mentioned Westrum."

The fat coroner belched, excused himself and looked intently into Black's eyes. "That's a problem."

"Yes, it is." Clay Black's mind drifted back to the old days when he had first come to the region. The old, awful feeling returned to the pit of his stomach. "And we can't let it happen."

"No. We can't." The now two most powerful men in the country had once been close friends. But over the years they had grown apart, each grabbing their part of the spoils. Now, differing interests and a distracted animosity kept them to themselves.

"I'll take care of it," Isac Karp offered his old friend. "It could ruin us both."

Clay Black only nodded. He had no taste for blood. At least, not anymore. "See you do." He turned and left. Chick followed.

"He'll screw it up," Chick said suddenly, breaking his silence as he rode next to Clay on their way back to the ranch.

"Maybe. But it's better he gets his hands bloody rather than me," Clay said almost in a whisper. "Mine are bloody enough." As they passed the town's new boot hill, another cemetery crossed his mind.

"Death is death," Chick answered. "It comes harder for some."

Chapter 7

Bolejack had about had his fill of Maggotwood. He had only come back to find some answers to questions that had long plagued his mind. It had also been to seek some nebulous revenge on those who had murdered his family. The red-hot anger of his childhood was gone now, only replaced with a dull numbness. He only had suspicions and vague dark memories to go on—no real evidence. Of course, the most obvious suspects were Clay Black and Isac Karp. They were the men who now controlled the land his father had once owned. Were they the men that had killed his family that terrible day? Most certainly, they were the ones who had come into possession of his father's land and holdings. He had also noted the fear roused at the very mention of King Westrum's name. But how could he prove anything?

He had been there sitting on the porch of Argent Hotel all morning. The hard wood of the chair was making his butt hurt. Hell, the whole town was making his butt hurt.

There was some shouting and then the swing doors of the Dead Carcass Saloon flung open and belched out some grizzled old gray-headed man adorned in dirty wooly chaps.

"And don't come back in here till you got some money!" growled Pock Johnson as he stood over the man. "No more credit!"

As the old man attempted to get to his feet, Pock Johnson drew back his leg and roughly kicked him sprawling face first down the porch steps and out into the dusty street.

Bolejack had already departed his chair and was out in the street as the old geezer unsuccessfully attempted to rise to his feet. "That's enough of that!" Bolejack warned.

Pock looked down from the steps at Bolejack surprised. A smug sneer then crossed his ugly face. "Seems you got a problem minding your own business," Pock said as he started to turn away. But Bolejack was already up on the porch of saloon jerking Pock's shoulder toward him. A big fist game out of nowhere and sent Pock crashing backwards through the batwings.

"I'm be switched," an onlooker exclaimed as the senseless bartender lay just inside the bar. "Never thought I'd see that—"

Bolejack stepped inside the saloon and stood holding the swinging doors as he gazed at the lifeless man. "Tell him he shouldn't bully old drunks over a drink," he told the stunned patrons of the bar.

Bolejack had seen the old man around town before, but hadn't paid much attention to him other than noticing he always pretended to be drunker than he really was. He stuck out his big hand to the man and helped him up.

"Thanks," the oddly dressed codger said meekly as he dusted his dirtied woolies off and adjusted his battered hat. Bolejack couldn't help but wonder why the old man still wore those hot old sheep-skin chaps in the summer.

"They call me Wooly. Wooly James," the ancient gent said as he wiped dirt from his wrinkled face.

"And I'm…."

"Bolejack," the old man said as a twinkle came to his face. "I know who you are. I know all about you."

Bolejack looked the ancient ruffian up and down, and somehow felt that he had seen him before.

"Do I know you?" Bolejack queried.

"Not now," the old man answered mysteriously, "not now. But sometime."

By now a small crowd had gathered around them and around the still unconscious barkeep. Bolejack turned around as loud steps along the gallery came closer. Isac Karp and a couple of his helpers stopped and stood by the door of the saloon looking in at the slowly reviving Pock Johnson. Then they turned their attention toward Wooly and Bolejack. Karp only nodded his head in recognition, but remained silent.

Bolejack turned back to the old man known as Wooly James. "Maybe you need to find another saloon old timer," he said as a smile crossed his face.

"There ain't no other saloon in this hole of a town," Wooly protested as he started to turn away. But then he turned back, and in a low voice said: "Tomorrow afternoon, one o'clock. The old Maggotwood boothill. Got something to show you."

"Show me?"

Then he was gone.

Chapter 8

Bolejack rode slowly out of town a little after twelve-thirty the next day. He noted that Isac Karp and several of his henchmen were watching.

In the back of his mind he wondered if he was being set up. He knew nothing about Wooly James. For all he knew, the old man could be leading him into a trap. He might even be working for Karp or even Clay Black. But there was nothing else he could do. He'd have to play his hand out.

Judging by the sun overhead, he arrived at the old cemetery just before one o'clock. He had been in no hurry and had stopped and smoked several times on the way. He was thinking things over.

There was no sign of Wooly James or anyone else. He sat there on his horse for a few minutes, but then dismounted and began to retrace the vague path he had recently left there in the weeds.

"You came," a voice said as if from thin air. Then he saw the old man up ahead standing near an old mule under a large tree.

"I did."

"Funny thing about boneyards," Wooly began. "We always put them out of our minds when we return to the living. It's only when we fear for our own mortality that we visit them again—as if to hold them at arm's length and reassure ourselves that we'll never wind up there. But that's not how it turns out, is it?"

Bolejack stared at the ancient man and once again had a feeling that he had known him in some other time or some other place. "I guess not," Bolejack finally said. It was only then that he noticed Wooly James was standing next to the grave marker of King Westrum. He had a shovel in one hand. Another shovel was leaning against the tombstone. "You're not going to…?"

"Dig him up?" Wooly completed his sentence. "Yes, I am, and so are you."

"Are you crazy?!" Bolejack said angrily as he came near him.

"Aren't we all… a little?"

"You damned—" Bolejack began as he started to draw his gun. "Stop!"

But Wooly James started digging. "This is what I want to show you."

Bolejack clicked back the hammer of his Colt, then stopped. "So, what's your game?" he choked out as he clicked back the gun's hammer and then slowly slid it back into his holster.

"The truth," Wooly said, "the truth never killed anybody, but lies do."

"This better all make sense or you're a dead man."

"We're all dead now or soon to be, ain't we?" Wooly winked as he continued digging.

Bolejack picked up the other shovel and reluctantly started to dig.

Six feet down they hit something. It was the casket.

"Dang it! I didn't come here to rob a grave! Especially my own father's!" Bolejack exploded as he threw the shovel down.

But the wiry old man had already inserted the tip of his shovel into the edge of the casket and began prying it open.

"For the love of…!" Bolejack moaned as he pulled out his weapon once again.

But then the lid of the casket creaked open with a rusty rasping sound and revealed a moldering mass of hay stuffed into a ragged old checkered shirt and holey bib overalls. Bricks had also been placed around the scarecrow to give the casket weight. The two men stood silently regarding the open casket.

"This is what I had to show you," Wooly said as he coughed and wearily leaned against the side of the hole. "You wouldn't have believed me otherwise."

"You knew Westrum wasn't buried here… but how?" Bolejack said in disbelief. "And the others…."

"May they rest in peace."

"But why? How?"

"That's something you'll come to know," the old man said cryptically. "I ain't got all the answers."

"Karp? Black? Someone else?"

"Like I said. I ain't sure about all that. That's why we have to cover this grave back up."

"I guess I don't understand."

"There's a lot you don't understand. But understand this. They're out to kill you. You're the nightmare that wasn't supposed to come back."

"But what do we do now?"

Wooly shrugged his stooped shoulders, slammed the casket lid down and began climbing out of the hole. "We go to Tombstone, Arizona. That's what we do. As soon as we fill in this hole."

"Tombstone? Why?"

"Yeah, well, you'll find out. And it sounds appropriate, don't it?"

Chapter 9

Bolejack didn't like being played for a fool. He wanted answers. As he followed behind the slow-moving mule that carried Wooly James, his mind was trying to bring together the scattered pieces of the mystery that was King Westrum. He had seen his father being dragged away with his own eyes. Could it be that he was still living? How and why could that be?

"The sun will be going down soon," Wooly called back.

"We'll make camp in an hour," Bolejack answered, distracted from his thoughts. If his father had not been killed along with his mother and brother, how had he escaped?

A few miles later they found a good spot to make camp. The sun's edge was just beginning to descend on the horizon as Wooly started a fire.

"I reckon you're wondering who I am and how I know so much," James began as he angled a pot of coffee over the fire.

"That has been crossing my mind," Bolejack said. He snapped off a chaw of old jerky he had retrieved from his saddlebag. It was the last piece he had. It was all he could do to chew the stringy meat. "I'd offer you some but…."

"Naw, thanks, I got a few old biscuits to eat." Bolejack stared at the dancing yellow flames as the sky grew gradually dark. "You were there, when they killed them, weren't you?"

A rare suppressed glint tried to break out across Wooly's leathered face as his dull gray and brown-stained teeth briefly gleamed in the fire light but then quickly vanished. "Yeah," he said, sobering, "I was there. And I'm still there in my mind. I heard all the commotion as I was riding back home. I saw them drag Westrum, his wife and your brother away. I wondered where you were. I knew your family. Good folks. That's why I couldn't figure it out at first."

"Figure what out?"

"Why they let your father go. And why he just stood there watching them as they dragged his wife and your brother around and not doing nothing to stop it."

"But I heard some men say they killed them all! But if they didn't kill Paw, why did they have that fake grave?"

A strange light came to Wooly's watery eyes. "Why, that was another odd thing. Yes, it was. They pretended there was three bodies, but it was just your maw and big brother and a dummy—a scarecrow you saw that they buried. The same one we just dug up!"

"That don't make any sense."

"No, it don't. But I saw it. And then I saw King Westrum sign some papers that Black and Karp had brought as they rode up. And damn if they didn't all shake hands. Just like some business deal. They even smiled!"

"I don't believe it!"

"But you better. Then I saw Westrum just get on his horse and ride away like nothing happened."

Bolejack sat silent, his eyes looking down into the dirt. The fire crackled loudly. "And all these years…."

"You know what else I heard?" Wooly gazed somberly at Bolejack. "I heard later that Westrum's was living high and mighty for years under a different name just outside of Tombstone—and that he's been coming back to these parts every now and then to raid and steal some of Black's cattle. They say he's even torched some of Karp's property."

Bolejack's eyes returned to the fire. "Do Black and Karp know you saw them that night?"

"Hell no. I've played the part of an old drunk for years now since my wife died. If they knew or even suspected, I'd be lying up there in their new boothill."

"So, they think I've come back to claim what used to be my father's land—and that I might be the one raiding them? And that's why they'll soon be after me."

"Son," Wooly said softly. "They're already after you."

Chapter 10

The next morning Bolejack woke to the sweet smell of bacon, biscuits and Arbuckle coffee. The sun was just beginning to peek over the distant jade trees as he regarded Wooly hunched over the campfire. Could he really be trusted, he wondered? It had been a long time since he had trusted anybody. The world was ripe with liars and lies. But still, sometime, somewhere, a man had to trust somebody.

"You gonna sleep all morning?" Wooly chided him as Bolejack stretched his long arms over his head and yawned.

"I'm just—"

A gun shot suddenly split the stillness of the new morning as both Wooly and Bolejack flattened themselves against the ground. A hole in the boiling coffee pot spewed brown liquid into the hissing fire.

"Put your hands up," a voice boomed as Bolejack yanked his Colt from under his saddle.

"Hell no!" Bolejack yelled as he rolled forward and came up shooting. His gun barked at two looming shadows near the tree line as more bullets kicked up dirt all around him. Then he heard the coach gun Wooly always carried explode. The shadows crumpled and there was silence.

Bolejack slowly walked toward the two dark figures motionless on the ground. Wooly was right behind him with one last barrel of buckshot still ready to explode.

"You know them?" Bolejack asked as his boot poked beneath one of the dead men's chest as he turned him over.

"Seems I might have seen them hanging around Maggotwood. Probably a couple of Karp's men," Wooly said as he lowered his gun.

"That's what I was thinking." Bolejack ejected his spent cartridges and reloaded. "Looks like you were right about them being after me."

Wooly James scratched his gray scraggly beard. "But I reckon I ain't got it all figured out. Something don't add up. There must be more to this story."

Bolejack sauntered back to the fire and picked up the riddled coffee pot. He shook it. "Must be a cup or two left," he announced as Wooly scooped up the burning bacon and biscuits.

"Danged if them boys didn't near spoil our breakfast," he mused. "And what if I can't figure why keeping Westrum a secret is so blamed important that they have to kill you—and me too!"

Bolejack only nodded as he poured himself a cup of coffee. Although it was beginning to make some sense with Wooly's explanations, there was still something missing to the puzzle.

"We have to find Westrum—dead or alive," he said matter-of-factly. "I want to know the why of all this. Then we'll go back to Maggotwood and deal with Karp and Black."

"Yup," Wooly muttered in is mustache, "them maggots in and around Maggotwood has got to pay." He bit into a burnt piece of bacon and looked back at the two dead men laying in the dust. "They got their pay."

Chapter 11

"It's been near a week," Clay Black snarled, "you heard from your boys yet?"

Karp shuffled his ponderous feet under the poker table as he looked up into the bleary eyes of the monarch of Black Cross Ranch. "You're interrupting my game. And no, I haven't heard from them. Quit pushing me. These things take time." Karp eyed the other two men at the table. They were both employed by him, so anything they heard would be safe.

Black gave him a look of disgust. "I'll give it one more week, Karp… and then I'll take care of it myself— with or without you."

"Suit yourself, but I expect I'll hear back from my boys in a few days. If not…"

"If not, you've got as much to lose as me." Black turned and angrily stomped out of the Dead Carcass.

"Boys," the corpulent Karp pondered, "that is one impatient man." They all laughed and then resumed their game.

Behind the bar, the stoic figure of Pock Johnson filed away the proceedings in the back of his mind. He had been the original owner of the Dead Carcass and had been there since the beginning of the town itself. He had reluctantly sold out his interest in the saloon but only with the stubborn stipulation that he could work there as head man for the rest of his life. Surprisingly, Karp had agreed. But even so, a tiny seed of resentment had been planted in Pock's mind over the years. It had even grown larger as he sat back and watched the growing tentacles of both Karp and Black ensnare the entire town and region. But what could he do? He was helpless. Then there was the thing with King Westrum. It had never sat well with him. It was unhealthy to even think about it, let alone talk about. He was surprised that Bolejack had even made it out of town alive after shooting his mouth off about Westrum. Others had died doing just that. But no matter, it would only be a short time now before Bolejack would turn up dead. Only the dead can speak of the dead.

It had been a longer ride than Bolejack had thought, but the sleepy and ragged town of Tombstone could be seen just up ahead. "The town's too tough to die, some say," Bolejack said out loud as he turned around in his saddle to watch Wooly James ride up behind him.

"I been there before," James said as he took a big swig of whisky from a bottle he magically pulled from his saddlebag. "It seemed pretty dead the last time I was here—but that was before the Earps. Course they're gone now."

Bolejack watched as Wooly took a second longer drink. "Where you been hiding that?"

"Oh, I had it all along. I only drink when a town's in sight—I never drink on the trail. Want a swallow?"

"Naw," Bolejack grinned, "not now. Maybe later."

"I think Westrum's place might be on the other side of Tombstone, but I ain't for sure. I just heard it was."

"We'll head on in to town and ask around."

"And maybe get a drink?"

"More?" Bolejack said, a slight smile still on his face. "Thought you might have had enough already."

"A man can't ever have too much—unless he has serious work or forgetting to do."

"Which we do. Work." Bolejack reminded him. "Westrum."

"You always take the fun out of things, boy. And his name around these parts is now Smith. Jasper Smith."

"Smith? Not too original."

"Nope." Wooly took off his hat and scratched his shaggy gray head. "Too bad them Earp boys pulled out. Heard they was something."

"I don't think we'll be needing much help from the law anyway."

"Naw, you're right. Revenge is the best law a man needs."

Chapter 12

Rose was worried about her father. She worried that he might someday learn the truth. The truth. That was always a worry. But he hadn't been the same since that man Bolejack had appeared. Something seemed to be bothering him deeply. She tried to remember if she had ever heard the name Westrum before. But it was no use. The name remained a mystery to her.

Her father had also been making more trips into town lately to see Isac Karp. She knew they had had business dealings over the years, but this seemed different. She had also noticed him staying up later at night and shuffling through papers at his desk—papers that he kept in a locked drawer. What could all this mean?

"I'll be going into town again, dear," her father remarked as he caught her giving him a quizzical look. "I've got more business to take care of."

"Yes, Father," she meekly answered as she began to turn away. But then she turned back and faced him head-on. "It wouldn't have anything to do with that Westrum fellow… or Bolejack, would it?"

She was set aback by the frightened look in her father's eyes. His face drained of its natural color. "Westrum?! Why… no. I don't even know any Westrum. And Bolejack? He's just some crazy drifter…."

"But I heard their names mentioned… and I thought—"

"Don't let it trouble you, dear," Clay Black replied, regaining his composure. "You must have heard some references to some old outlaw or something. There's no one by the name of Westrum around here anymore."

Rose Black nodded and again turned away. "Have a good trip Father."

"I will," Clay murmured under his breath. As Rose walked away, her father completed the sentence in a low, barely audible snarl, "when Westrum and Bolejack rot in hell…."

Chapter 13

"So, this is the famous Crystal Palace," Bolejack said as he and Wooly James entered. "It's not all that much to look at."

"Looks like they're letting it get run down," Wooly added. "The girls, too, by the looks of them."

"Dang," Bolejack said, "I don't know what all the fuss is about Tombstone anyway. Just another cow town with your usual scum of the earth and overly soiled doves."

"It do seem that way, but even so, it's a big step up from Maggotwood."

"More saloons, gamblers and gals anyway."

The bar was about half full as Bolejack and Wooly eased up to it. The bartender was a big-shouldered middle-aged gent with a shiny head, walrus mustache and jowls of a bemused bulldog.

"What's your choice, boys?"

"Whiskey," Bolejack said.

"You got any cold beer?" Wooly asked.

"Coldest in town," the barkeep said.

With drinks in hand, the two weary travelers eyed the motely collection of humanity scattered around the room. A rail-thin man in a frayed brown suit, scruffy sweater, crumpled felt hat and over-large starched collar stood a few feet away regarding them.

"Sir," Bolejack politely began, "is there a ranch nearby owned by a mister Jasper Smith? We heard on the trail that he's hiring hands, so we thought we'd ride through town and ask around."

The skinny man looked at Bolejack suspiciously, but then seemed to suddenly warm up to him. His eyes, slightly cocked, seemed to swivel toward him and Wooly.

"Antrim. Antrim's the name," he said as he smiled and stuck out his hand. "William."

"I'm Bolejack and this here's Wooly James—no relation to Jesse." He held out his big paw and was surprised by the strength of the skinny fellow's grip.

"Oh, yes… mister Smith… I'm afraid I'veggot bad news. Mister Smith is dead. A few months ago, I suppose. I tried to hire on there myself, but he had just died."

"Dead?"

"Yes—as they say out here so adroitly: dead by lead poisoning."

"I see."

"But the ranch is still in operation, so they may need some help. I've gone on to other work, as they say. The ranch is about two miles east of town."

Bolejack shook his head as he noticed the large gun strapped to the skinny runt's side.

"But who's running the Smith place now?"

The young Mr. Antrim took a drink of his beer. Then he smiled and revealed two large buck teeth. "I'm not sure exactly who runs it now, but I've heard it's owned by the Black Cross Ranch."

"Need another drink?" the bulldog bartender asked.

Bolejack put a double eagle on the bar. "Nope. That will do it."

As Bolejack and Wooly turned to leave, the crumple-hatted youngster thanked them for paying for his beer. "And you can just call me Billy…."

Chapter 14

Bolejack and Wooly looked back over their shoulders at the dimming amber lights of Tombstone as they headed east. It seemed that the mystery of King Westrum only deepened the more they tried to unravel it. They slowly passed a few ramshackle shacks, but encountered no other riders. The sun had gone down, and darkness swooped over them quickly. A cluster of lights up ahead soon appeared.

"That must be the ranch," Wooly volunteered.

Bolejack only grunted and nodded. "We'll skirt around it and look for any graves," he finally said. "No need to make our presence known unless we have to."

The entrance of the place was marked by a large arching overhead sign. But whatever had once announced the ranch's title had been pulled down, and in its place was a poorly painted wood placard simply stating: Black Cross Ranch II.

"Let's head around to the right," Bolejack said. Not knowing the exact dimensions of the ranch, they followed the wire fencing. The ranch land and fencing seemed to never end.

"I say the hell with it!" Wooly exclaimed after what seemed like several miles of endless wandering. "We could be riding the perimeter of this thing all night and all day tomorrow."

Bolejack had pulled up his horse and sat thinking. He squinted into the darkness. "Just a little longer," he said as he urged his tired horse ahead.

About a half hour later, Wooly, exasperated and a little saddle sore, had had it. "We need to make camp for the night! It ain't all that long till dawn."

"Up ahead, to the left of that rise," Bolejack replied.

Wooly James strained his eyes as he looked up ahead. Only a half moon provided any light.

"But that's on the other side of the fencing," he sighed.

"Come on," Bolejack said as his dark red horse wearily trotted on ahead. "Now look… closer."

Wooly blinked his sleepy eyes and pretended to not see what was up ahead. "Is that a… tombstone?"

Bolejack was off his horse. He fished out a pair of wire cutters from his saddlebag, walked over to the fencing and began cutting the wire.

"They ain't gonna like that," Wooly offered.

As they approached the single pale stone, a cool night wind came off the arid land and rustled the sparse trees that surrounded the site. Bolejack paused as the vague feeling that he had done this before in his dreams overcame him.

"It says Jasper Smith," he said numbly. "It's him. But I guess we better make sure." He walked back to his horse and untied the short shovel he had strapped to his saddle.

"You're not…"

"Yes I am."

Bolejack bent grimly to his task. "You could help. You seem to like doing this sort of thing."

"No shovel," Wooly replied, a slight crooked smile crossing his lips.

Bolejack grunted and dug harder. His back ached as he strained to complete the job. Luckily, his shovel struck wood only three feet down.

"Looks like they were in a hurry," he flatly stated. "No man should be buried less than six feet down."

Wooly watched the proceedings from his makeshift bed. He had hastily made camp and bedded down while Bolejack dug and had even started a small fire.

"Those Black Cross boys might see that," Bolejack complained.

"Might."

Bolejack's shovel pried at the top of the cheap pine box that held Westrum's body. The screeching nails sounded like wounded coyotes wailing in the night as the lid slowly came off.

Bolejack ripped open the wood casket, flung the lid to one side and stared at its contents. He couldn't believe what he was seeing.

Wooly sat up slightly on one elbow, his curiosity aroused. But he didn't bother to get up and look. Somehow, he seemed to know the contents of the pine box.

"So?" Wooly finally asked.

Bolejack angrily reached down into the wood oblong box and pulled up the flimsy remains of a badly-made scarecrow. He cursed the night.

"It seems Westrum never dies!" Bolejack hissed as he slung the straw man back down into the casket.

"I'm turning in," Wooly answered calmly as the fire from the campfire began to dim. "Mr. Westrum makes me tired."

Chapter 15

When they rode off the next morning, Bolejack didn't bother reburying the straw effigy he had dug up. He'd had it with moldering scarecrows.

But as they slowly rode away, several men on horseback could be seen riding toward them in the distance.

"Where we going?" Wooly asked as they rode out.

"Back to Maggotwood!" Bolejack shouted back at him as their horses broke into a gallop. "But we'll stop and see Clay Black first."

"I need a drink."

"Out already?"

"Yeah," Wooly shouted back. "All this riding makes a man awful thirsty."

The men they had seen from a distance seemed to vanish as they rode hard toward the northwest. They decided to ride past Tombstone even though Wooly complained again about needing a drink.

When they camped that night, Bolejack pulled a half-full bottle of Old Overholt from his saddlebag.

"Been saving this for you," he said as he tossed it to Wooly.

"You had me worried," the old man said as he smiled. "I was starting to get the jitters. Not that I'm an overly hard-drinking man…"

"No fire tonight," Bolejack said as he began to unsaddle. "Or tomorrow morning."

Somehow the night seemed warmer as they turned in. Wooly seemed quieter than usual as he nursed his bottle. Bolejack slowly nodded off when he heard the clink of the empty Overholt bottle. Wooly had only offered him one from the bottle. But that was all right. Bolejack leaned back and listened to the snoring of the old man as he slowly drew his revolver from its holster and gently tucked it under his saddle. Then the darkness became total.

But dreams crowded into Bolejack's sleep, dreams of men digging up graves, shots being fired, bloody things dragged endlessly behind horses. The smiling long faces of coyotes seemed to loom above him, paw at the moist dirt that he suddenly realized surrounded him as he jerked upright clawing at the lid of the coffin above him—"

Again, a shot broke the silence of the night and the nightmare. Was it still the dream?

"What…?" Bolejack bolted upright and then, out of instinct, rolled to one side and clutched for the gun under his saddle. It wasn't there. He rose, panicked, and dove at the rifle he had leaned against a rock. The spark and sting of rock chips made him jerk his hand away from the rifle but then he grabbed for it again, aimed at the darkness and fired wildly. Something, an animal or man, screamed. Then there was silence.

Bolejack shifted his eyes in the darkness toward where Wooly had been sleeping. He was gone.

Another shot rang out, but this one was away from the camp.

"You all right?" Wooly asked as he came trotting out of the blackness. "I think you winged one of them!"

"Who was it? Could you tell?"

"Couldn't get a good look. I just woke up after I heard a noise and saw somebody standing over you with a gun. He got spooked and took off running when he saw me. Then somebody else started shooting!"

"The Black Cross bunch I reckon," Bolejack said as he flopped back down on his saddle.

"I reckon," Wooly agreed. He handed Bolejack his Colt. "I found it after I chased that feller. Got blood on it."

Bolejack wiped it on his shirt and holstered it. "Thanks."

Next morning the pale, yellow edge of sun split sharply over the far rim of the ragged horizon. An inkling of torn clouds moved sluggishly in the sky.

"It's about time to get up," Wooly mused aloud as he scratched his gray and white bearded chin. "Seemed like a short night." He started to get the fixings out for breakfast, but he wasn't looking forward to a cold fireless meal. He turned around to make sure Bolejack was looking away. Then he pulled a rag from his saddlebag and wiped some of the still-wet oozing blood away from the bullet crease on the back of his leg. Most of it had already dried. He'd been lucky, he told himself. Mighty lucky.

Chapter 16

"I should shoot you right off that horse!" the bristling foreman of the Black Cross Ranch said. "You got your nerve coming back here."

"I just got to missing you, Chick," Bolejack sarcastically answered as he tried to hold back a smile.

"What'd you want?"

"I need to talk to Clay Black. There seems to be a misunderstanding."

It was the middle of the afternoon, and Bolejack was dead tired from riding. He and Wooly sat calmly at the south gate entrance of Black Cross land.

Chick Swickard lowered his rifle as did the men behind him. He knew that Black wanted Bolejack dead. But the old drunk riding with Bolejack complicated things. There was a limit to how far he would go when it came to following Black's orders. He didn't want to hang for murder or be forced to kill them both. He'd crossed his moral limit a couple of times already and had always regretted it. He wouldn't cross it again if he could help it. Black would have to call this shot.

"Okay," Chick said as he sighed, "ride on in, but remember we'll be right behind you."

"Obliged," Bolejack said as he made a mockery of tipping his hat.

Always two cocksure of himself, Chick thought to himself as they headed toward the ranch. But still he couldn't make himself truly hate him even though he knew he was a possible rival for Rose's affection. But she'd see through him eventually—see him for the drifter he was, and even if she didn't, he expected it to only be a short-term problem. Black or Karp would see to that.

As they approached the huge stone and frame main ranch house, Black was just hitching his horse to the tie rail. He'd apparently been out riding and had just returned.

"Josie!" he yelled at one of the ranch hands as they approached, "put up my horse and rub her down good."

Bolejack noticed that Rose Black had leisurely drifted out on the porch as they rode up to the now rigid and determined Clay Black. He stood there immobile and silent with his hands on his hips as Bolejack and Wooly dismounted.

"Your boys weren't much count," Bolejack belligerently said as he stopped in front of Black.

"My boys?"

"Yeah, the ones you sent to shoot us."

A strange smile flashed across Black's face, then quickly melted away. "You're wrong," Black whispered, "they weren't my boys—if they'd been my boys we wouldn't be talking now."

"Maybe that narrows it down," Bolejack said as the bloated image of Isac Karp flitted across his mind. "But I'm still looking and asking."

"About what?"

"Westrum."

Rose Black had descended from the long wraparound porch and was now standing beside her father. "You seem obsessed with this Mr. Westrum," Rose offered.

"I suppose I am, ma'am," Bolejack answered, trying not to dwell on her more than the adequate bosom that now gently rose and fell beneath her tight blouse.

"This doesn't concern you, dear," her father said grimly. "And it most certainly doesn't concern you either, Mr. Bolejack."

"Oh, but it does!" Bolejack said loudly as Chick twitched to attention behind him. "You see, I'm Bill… William Westrum. The one that got away all those years ago!"

Black's face went pale as he staggered slightly back "It can't be—he's dead—and you call yourself Bolejack!"

"Yes… Bolejack's my name now. It's the name of some kind folks that took me in. But I'm really Bill Westrum, not Bill Bolejack."

"Get off my land!" Black screamed. "Chick, escort these two off the ranch—and if they refuse—shoot them!"

"That still doesn't answer my question," Bolejack growled as he lurched forward and grabbed Black by his shirt. "Where's Westrum?! We dug up two graves where he was supposed to be buried and there was no body!"

The iron barrel of Chick's gun crashed heavily across the back of Bolejack's head as Black jerked himself free.

"Shoot him! Shoot them both!" Black screamed in rage.

Wooly had pulled out his gun but was quickly disarmed by two of the Black Cross men. He spat in their faces.

"Shoot them? Here? Now?" Chick hesitated. "That would be murder."

"You can't, Dad!" Rose cried as she knelt over the prone figure of Bolejack. "Chick's right!"

Black had now drawn his own gun and clicked back the hammer.

"No!" Rose screamed as she threw herself over Bolejack.

Black eased back the hammer of his pistol and slowly slid it into its holster. "Take them off Black Cross land and… dump them! And if either one ever sets foot on my land again; they'll be shot on sight!"

Rose went running and crying back to the house as Chick and his men put Bolejack and Wooly on their horses. *'No stomach,'* Clay Black thought to himself as he regarded his sheepish foreman. *'He's got no stomach for killing anyone. It's not like back in the old days.'*

As they began to ride away, Black turned to Josie. "Tell Vonnie I need to talk to him." *'Vonnie. Vonnie Lynch. Now there's a man with a stomach for killing.'*

Chapter 17

Bolejack had regained consciousness by the time they were on the edge of Black Cross land. He then realized he was lying belly-down across his saddle and quickly scooted off the slowly trotting horse. He fell clumsily into the sand and cactus as he tried to pull out his phantom gun.

"You look a little silly playing in the sand," Chick observed as he and his cowhands chuckled. Wooly sat stoically on his horse unsmiling.

Chick tossed him his gun. "And just in case you didn't hear. The boss said you and your pal will be shot the next time you set foot here."

Bolejack rose to his full height as he brushed himself off. He holstered his gun and glared defiantly at the Black Cross men. "And I suppose you don't know anything about Westrum either."

"Nope."

Bolejack slid his boot into his horse's stirrup and glided into the saddle. "Let's get out of here, Wooly," he said. "Maybe Karp knows something."

It seemed like a long way to town for some reason as the two men rode on silently. Bolejack wasn't used to taking no for an answer, and it sure didn't sit well with him now. This whole Westrum thing was something he couldn't quite savvy.

It was starting to get dark when they rode into Maggotwood. Wooly had already turned off and gone back to his little shack at the north end of town. He had wished Bolejack luck and said he was tired. He was quitting. He was done with it all.

As Bolejack led his horse into the livery, he eyed the Dead Carcass Saloon across the street. It was busy as usual. He had thought about barging in there and confronting Karp first thing. But his head had began throbbing again from Chick's clubbing, and suddenly every bone in his body was aching. He'd talk to Karp tomorrow. Right now, all he wanted to do was to check in at the hotel and get a good night's rest.

As he signed the registry in the Argent Hotel, he noticed a greasy little man in the lobby watching him. It was no doubt one of Karp's men. It could have been one of the Black Cross hires too, but he doubted it. There was nothing in the small man's demeanor that denoted a cowhand—he had more the air of a failed gambler or a back shooter.

But the seedy little fellow soon dissolved from Bolejack's thoughts as he settled back in the hotel's big featherbed. He carefully slung his holster over a brass rail post, but then removed the gun. Over the years he had learned that his revolver was his best bed partner.

As sleep slowly descended upon him, the mystery of Westrum—the whole who and why of it all swirled through his head. Who really was this Westrum? He had to be more than just his father. None of it made sense. And why was it so important that people needed to think he was dead? As these questions slowly dissolved away in his mind, the creak of a window suddenly woke him. He could see a small figure step into the dark room. Almost by instinct he rolled to the side of the bed away from the window and onto the floor as the two shots riddled the bed. Quickly, he rose from his knees and fired. Glass shattered from the window panes but the man was gone. Bolejack ran to the window and saw a figure hitting the street below him. He fired again, but only sand and dirt puffed up as the stranger escaped. Was it the greasy little gent that had watched him in the lobby? It was too dark to tell. *'Hell,'* Bolejack thought, what does a guy have to do to get some sleep anymore?

Chapter 18

The sickly orange sun was three fingers high above the hazy horizon when Bolejack woke up. He hadn't intended to sleep that late. He went quickly about his morning chore of shaving as he grimaced into the cracked mirror. Briefly, he toyed with the idea of letting his mustache grow out again, but then he lathered up his upper lip and scraped it smooth. The straight-edged razor seemed to drag and catch at his skin. It was dull. He'd have to strop it soon.

Breakfast at the attached hotel café was uneventful, and the food was only fair to middling. The pale eggs seemed far from fresh. There was no hurry in his step as he approached the Dead Carcass Saloon. As he neared the door he hesitated and then kept walking right past it. He continued walking down past a shabby little cigar store that sported a weathered wooden Indian whose once large nose had been whittled away. He kept walking.

He had just passed a colorful millenary shop when he heard someone say his name. He stopped.

"Mr. Bolejack?!" a woman's voice repeated out of nowhere. He turned and saw Rose Black emerge from the store. "I thought that was you," she said as she hurried up to him. "I'm so sorry about how Father treated you yesterday…."

Bolejack tipped his hat slightly and smiled. "No need ma'am, sometimes I can come across a little brash."

"But it was wrong!" she exclaimed, "all you did was ask a question."

"That doesn't seem to be a popular thing to do around here."

"No. I guess not." She turned to walk away but then turned back. "If I knew anything, I'd tell you—but it's all a mystery to me too."

"Thank you anyway, ma'am."

"And… I'd like to see you again."

"That might not be healthy."

Rose smiled and once again turned away. "But you're not much on your health, are you?"

Bolejack didn't answer, he just stood there watching the soft rhythmic sway of her hips as she walked away.

"I guess not," he whispered to himself as he started up again. On the next block he stopped and looked in the window of a gun shop. He stood there several minutes gazing upon the new and second-hand guns that lined the window. The owner inside eyed him suspiciously.

This wasn't like him, he told himself—hesitating when there was a job to do. Was he losing his nerve? Or was all this not that important? He turned around and headed back toward the Dead Carcass.

He could hear the off-key tinkle of the piano before he brushed past the greasy saloon doors. The din momentarily died down slightly as strange twisted faces looked up from the gaming tables and the half-filled bar. Then all the faces snapped back, and the soft rumble of the saloon resumed.

Bolejack cautiously ambled toward the bar looking for anyone familiar. There was none. Isac Karp was nowhere in sight. Even the familiar ugly mug of Pock Johnson was not to been seen.

"Where's Pock?" Bolejack asked the strange thin bartender.

"His day off," the man said. "You want a drink?"

"Whiskey." Bolejack watched the odd small-headed man as his reedy long arms poured the whiskey. *'Damn if he don't remind me of a big praying mantis,'* he thought to himself. "Is Mr. Karp here today?"

"Who's asking?" the emaciated barkeep said without seemingly moving the mouth in his tiny head.

"Bolejack."

"I'll see if he's busy."

The queer insect-like man disappeared. A second average-sized barkeep that Bolejack had never seen before slowly polished glasses while staring at him.

Finally, the bug-headed saloon man reappeared. "He can see you now. He's upstairs. First door on the left."

Bolejack threw back his head and drained the shot glass. He plinked down the payment and walked toward the stairs. As he went up the creaking steps, he felt several sets of eyes on him.

At the top of the stairs he tapped lightly on the door, then instinctively slid to one side. A loud shotgun blast splintered the door as Bolejack lost his footing and fell back. His hand jerked up with his gun firing.

As the smoke cleared, there was silence. Bolejack rose stiffly, then cautiously peered into the room. It was empty. The window was open as a strong breeze stirred the curtains. He went to the window and looked out. He noted a walkway along the window's edge. It was empty.

As he descended the stairs, the praying mantis barkeep looked at him blankly. Bolejack, his gun still in hand, sauntered up to the slick bar and walloped the bug man across his face. He let out a high shrill squeal as he disappeared behind the bar.

"I guess Mr. Karp had another appointment," Bolejack said as he turned away. "I'll catch him next time."

Chapter 19

The street was strangely quiet when Bolejack brushed pass the swing doors. In most towns the sound of gunfire would bring the townspeople running—but not here. Not in Maggotwood.

He slowly walked back toward the hotel. What was Isac Karp hiding? Was he one of the men that had dragged his mother and brother to their deaths? Wooly had thought so. And had his father paid them off for his own life, but not the lives of his family? Was he that evil?

A shot suddenly buzzed past Bolejack's right ear. He dove behind a water barrel as he drew his gun. There was silence, and then the muted sound of someone running away. A warm sensation made him bring his hand to his ear. Blood. The bullet had nicked his ear.

"You all right?" a familiar voice asked from the veranda of the Argent Hotel.

"Yeah, just a crease."

"I could see him running north," Pock Johnson said as he leaned back in his chair. "Thought I could hear some shooting down by the Dead Carcass, too. But that ain't my concern right now—it's my day off."

"So I see." Bolejack entered the hotel and went up to his room. He had some thinking to do. The pieces to the puzzle of King Westrum now seemed more scattered than ever.

The next day Bolejack rose late again and then leisurely strolled toward the north edge of town. A new large canvas tent caught his eye. A crudely painted wood plank sign by the tent's entrance announced its purpose: Wet Gulch Saloon. For some reason the north end of Maggotwood had always been known as the gulch—probably because of a story about two old prospectors being drygulched there during the early years of the town's existence.

The interior of Maggotwood's newest and second saloon was crude: three wooden beer barrels topped by two wide pine boards with a hodge-podge of half-broken second-hand poker tables and chairs strewn randomly around the dark enclosure.

"Was wondering when you'd find this place," Wooly James said in a low slurred voice. "They threw me out of the Dead Carcass."

"We both won't be too popular in there for a while," Bolejack said. He motioned to the barkeep. "A whiskey—make that two."

Wooly looked out over the motley patrons of the Dry Gulch. "I been asking around."

"And…?"

"Nobody wants to talk about Westrum—or they don't know nothing about him. That was a long time ago."

"But if he's not dead?"

"Then I guess he'll have to give us the answers."

Chapter 20

It was just after noon of the next day. Bolejack had left Wooly at the Wet Gulch Saloon the day before and returned to the hotel. The night was uneventful and he had turned in early. Now here he was leaning back in his low-backed chair on the porch of the Argent doing nothing. He had decided to stay away from the Dead Carcass for now. But he was thinking about riding back to the Black Cross Ranch again even though he knew it might be suicide.

At the far end of town, he casually watched a rider coming closer and closer. It looked like a woman. As the rider drew nearer, he suddenly tensed. It was Rose Black. She hurriedly pulled her horse up short near the hitch rack and got off.

"I need to talk to you," she said grimly. "Somewhere in private." There was an urgency in her voice.

"I'd invite you up to my room but…"

"That would be improper," she finished his sentence. "And someone might see us together. I'll ride out to the old boot hill and wait for you."

"I'll follow you out in about ten minutes."

Then she was gone.

Bolejack settled back in his chair. He was in no hurry. He wondered what was on her mind. After a few minutes he walked slowly to the livery and saddled up. On the way out he caught a glimpse of Wooly James watching him from a chair in front of St. John's Barber Shop. He pretended to not see him.

As he neared boot hill, his mind skipped like a stone on water at the memory of his parents, and at the bogus grave of King Westrum. Then he saw Rose's horse tied to a remnant of the old iron fence that once encircled the graveyard.

"There you are," Rose's voice drifted up to him from the other side of a large old gnarled mesquite. She appeared suddenly and walked toward him slowly. "I was afraid—afraid they'd stopped you somehow."

"They've been trying."

Rose was suddenly in his arms. He gently lifted her chin and looked into her dark eyes. They brimmed with tears.

"What's wrong?" he asked as he drew his face closer.

"I thought they might have killed you," she said. It was then, for the first time, he kissed her.

"I'm all right," he said softly as he drew slightly back, studying her eyes.

"My father—" she began. "I just don't know him anymore. It's like he's become another person." She reached down and pulled something from her pocket as she drew back. "And then I found this!"

Bolejack took the folded yellow documents from her hand.

"It's the old deeds to the Black Cross Ranch and the acreage that makes up Maggotwood," she explained. "I found them while looking in my father's desk. They were locked in a drawer. But I had remembered seeing the key to it hidden away when I was a child."

Bolejack shifted the papers carefully in his hands as he read them. "They're both signed by your father, Isac Karp and… King Westrum."

"Yes," Rose said quietly.

"But this still doesn't explain why he signed over his property—it sure wasn't for the lives of his wife and sons…."

"And it doesn't answer the question of what happened to him, either. Does it?" Rose said tonelessly. Then she was silent as her lips pressed against his.

Chapter 21

Bolejack knew what he had to do. Rose rode to the right of his blood red horse as they made their way to Black Cross Ranch. This time he'd get some answers from Clay Black one way or the other. Even is he had to shoot him.

Chick was perched atop the main corral near the house when Rose and Bolejack boldly rode up. He had a nasty smirk on his face. Several cowhands of the Black Cross were also scattered around, apparently watching a horse being broken.

"You got some nerve, Bolejack," Chick said as he eased off the fence and spat out a wad of tobacco. His hand went to his gun. "I should shoot you right now!"

"It's all right, Chick," Rose intervened.

"Well, I said it ain't! Your dad said…."

Bolejack had tied his horse to the edge of the corral and stood eying the red-faced foreman. Rose remained on her horse.

Chick swaggered up to Bolejack with a snarling possum grin on his face. The next instant Chick found himself sprawled backward in the dirt by the swift and powerful arch of Bolejack's rock-hard fist.

"What the—" Chick exclaimed as he wiped the blood from his mouth. Cat-like, he scrambled to his feet and lunged.

"Stay down," Bolejack said mechanically as he drove his left hand into Chick's face a second time. Then he jabbed sharply with a right-hand sending Chick teetering back like a drunken man.

"That's enough!" Clay Black's voice boomed behind Bolejack.

Bolejack spun around and stared into Clay's .45.

"I just wanted to talk to you."

"I told you I'd shoot you the next time. You're not welcome here!"

"I know that. But I still need answers."

"Some questions shouldn't be asked," Black said grudgingly. "Did you bring him back here?" he said as he looked up at the frightened pale face of his daughter.

She was silent a moment, then the color returned to her cheeks. "I did!" she suddenly blurted out, almost angrily. "I didn't want to snoop—but I had to know! I found these deeds locked in your desk—and I showed him!"

"You—" but he didn't complete his thought. His own face had turned dark and gloomy.

"They're co-signed by King Westrum," Bolejack said as he watched Chick slink away. "But the question remains—where's Westrum? He's not buried where he's supposed to be."

Clay Black flushed and then shivered. He slowly slid his Colt back in its holster. "I'd heard the rumors—but never believed them."

"The rumors he was alive and living near Tombstone?" Bolejack prodded.

"Yeah. But you know how stories like that are…."

"I know. And I know you're lying," Bolejack said flatly. "That's why I checked it out."

"And…."

"And you know the answer to that, too, don't you?" He studied Black's face closely as the old man recovered his composure and muted rage flickered across his wrinkled face.

"I don't know what you mean."

Bolejack walked toward Black, his years of frustration and anger suddenly boiling to the surface.

The soft click of gun hammers broke the silence like a chorus of cicadas on a summer evening. "You stop right there!" Chick Swickard hissed as he leveled his gun. Several of the other hands had also pulled their guns. "We warned you once already!"

"Stop it!" Rose screamed as she jerked her horse toward Chick, knocking him and two of the other hands over. "Just stop it!"

Bolejack sprung onto his own horse and took off.

"Get him!" Clay shouted as he fired wildly, but Bolejack was gone by the time Chick had scrambled back to his feet. A shot from the retreating rider sent the Black Cross hands diving for cover.

"Damn it!" Clay screamed as he leveled his gun at again at Bolejack. But Rose pulled her horse into him and continued to block his aim.

"Why?! Why are you doing this?" she screamed at her father. He roughly grabbed her by her arm and pulled her down.

"It's all for you child! All for you and us!" he choked out amid the dust and confusion.

"No! No, it's not!" Rose screamed back as her eyes filled with tears. "It's always been for you! Just you!"

Chapter 22

Bolejack thundered his horse across the ravine and then urged it up the incline a few miles outside of Black Cross. They would be after him now for sure, he reasoned, and they'd probably be headed by Clay Black himself. But was Black the real power here, or was it really Karp? Something still didn't quite jive in his mind. Even with his new knowledge of the old deeds, there was still a missing piece. Perhaps several missing pieces.

Maggotwood could be seen up ahead, but he had no time or desire to enter that hell hole again. He turned his horse south. He'd head for Mexico. That was the only thing he could come up with for the moment. He needed time to think and regroup. He had thought he would find all the answers here, but he had been foolish. The answers were buried too deep, too long. All he had for his efforts were two empty graves.

Bolejack was now well past Maggotwood. He stopped and turned slowly in his saddle to look back. The light of day was dying in the west. The town now seemed distant, just a row of small jagged brown teeth on the horizon.

'They've beaten me,' he heard himself thinking as the trail ahead dimmed in the darkness. It was like taking a swig of poison, and it was hard to swallow. Damn it! But what else could he do? Only Rose and Wooly had given him any help and encouragement. Everyone else had only

wanted him to go away and better yet drop dead. It was like the land itself wanted to guard its secret.

He rode on a few more miles lost in his gloomy thoughts. But it was time to make camp now. It would be pointless and dangerous to ride on into the mouth of the swallowing night.

When Clay Black rode into Maggotwood, it was with a purpose. He led an entourage of ten of his best men including Chick Swickard. They had tracked Bolejack to the north end of town and taken note that he had skirted it and headed on south. Black had ordered two of his men to follow Bolejack while he and rest of them rode on into town.

The Dead Carcass Saloon was a bubbling hive of activity. They had no trouble finding Isac Karp. He was vigorously commanding the biggest table in the establishment. The saloon went suddenly quiet when Black and his men filed noisily through the swinging doors. All eyes were upon them.

Karp, frowning at the disruption of his poker game, looked annoyed. Then his face took on an air of anticipation as he placed his cards face-down on the table. "This better be important," he grumbled.

"It is," Black shot back as he loomed at the far end. "We've got Bolejack on the run."

"So?"

"So, we have to get him now. He knows too much. And he's got the deeds."

Karp stood up and motioned to three of his boys nearby. "I see. Come on back to the office. This game is over."

In a far corner, Wooly James nursed a rye whiskey he had ordered an hour ago. He had sneaked quietly into the bar earlier, gotten a drink from one of the new bartenders who didn't know him and hidden in a dark corner of the bar. He now turned his wobbly and seemingly drunken countenance toward Karp's upstairs office as Black and Swickard followed Karp up the stairs. The remainder of Black's men gathered around the bar and ordered drinks.

When the door was closed, Karp turned around angrily and confronted Black. "What do you mean by prancing in here and spouting off about Bolejack in front of the whole saloon? You know we don't talk about him or Westrum in public!"

"I know," Black replied coldly, "but I had to get your attention. We've both cat-footed around this Bolejack character for too long. He could bring us all down and you know that!"

Karp pulled out a long black cigar, bit the end off and spat it at Black. "So why haven't you gotten rid of him? I've tried. And now you're saying I haven't done enough and that he's gotten away?"

"I've got two men following him now, and Vonnie Lynch."

"I suspect that won't do it. I'm not sure if even Lynch can take him."

"That's why I'm here. He talks like some tough monkey, but he's on the run now. I think he's lost his nerve. We're going after him even if he hightails it to Mexico. We can't have him out there asking questions and maybe coming back." Black nervously ran his fingers through his graying hair. "I've got twelve men, but I want you and some of your men, too. We should be in this together—like it or not."

"Wouldn't that be a little bit of an overkill?" Karp said as he crinkled up his forehead and puffed deeply on his cigar. "It's just one man we're after… unless you still think…."

"No. I don't. We buried him—twice. And then paid him off—twice. He'd better not try that again or a third time will be…."

"The charm—or the cure?" Karp quipped as something akin to a smile crossed his puffy lips. "But Bolejack's just a man. An honest man. And that's why he'll die."

"Maybe. Maybe not," Black said cryptically. "He's no ordinary man."

"I guess it runs in the blood—just like his old man."

"That's what I'm thinking now. And I'm afraid he'll be coming back to claim what's his, if we don't stop him."

"The hell…" Karp murmured. "We've put up with this for years. Dead men. Dead cattle. Buildings burnt. We kept up our bargain—he didn't. Damn Westrum… we should have killed them all when we had our chance years ago. How many times do we need to kill him!? Now this!"

Clay Black just stood there as Chick squirmed behind him. He sighed. "Well?"

"I'll saddle up and get eight of my best men ready."

"This IS important," Black said quietly as he turned and started to leave.

Karp crushed out his half-smoked Havana. "Important?" he coughed. "It's everything!"

Chapter 23

Rose Black hadn't left her room since her father had rode off with his men. She knew what their purpose was, and she could feel an unreasonable hate building up deep within her. She had always loved and respected this man she called her father, especially after her mother's death. There had been the usual teenage rebellions against him, but she had always returned to follow him even when she felt his decisions were wrong or cruel. But things were different now—she was a grown woman and now unwilling to blindly believe in him. And besides, she held the secret close to her heart that even Clay Black did not know. Her mother had revealed it on her death bed. She had lived with it ever since.

Rose sat silently in the room that had been her haven since her childhood. She had left untouched most of the now childish touches that her mother had made to her room. She hadn't had the heart to change things.

Now she carefully rolled up some of her clothes and personal items in the thick horse blanket she had spread out on her bed. Her saddlebag was also stuffed full. The cook had prepared some basic provisions for her. They were waiting for her on the dining room table just as she had requested.

"Your dad ain't gonna like this," Josh Barnes said as he led Rose's saddled horse from the barn.

"I'm surprised you didn't go with him," Rose said as she started to tie her belongings to the horse.

"Somebody had stay and watch the ranch and you," Josh said sourly. "I'd just as soon gone, but me and Gil and some of the other boys were told to stay here."

Rose didn't answer.

"Here, let me help you," Josh offered. "Maybe I should ride along with you—if anything was to happen to you…."

"I'll be fine."

Josh watched sadly as Rose rode off. He'd catch hell for letting her go when Clay got back. But what was he supposed to do? She was the daughter of the boss and all grown-up to boot. He couldn't stop her.

Bolejack's neck was starting to get a little sore from looking back so much. He knew they were coming, but he still hadn't seen them. He had stopped on a ridge overlooking the dry sandy basin he had just rode over. He pulled out a pack of cigarette papers and a yellowed bag of tobacco. Slowly, he sprinkled tobacco into the curled brown paper and built a smoke as his eyes scanned the basin. There was no sign of water here, but otherwise, it looked like a good place to camp for the night. To the west, the bright copper coin of sun began to edge down.

It was a warm night. He quickly set up a cold camp knowing that any fire would be a beacon for those in pursuit. After staring off into the dark nothingness for an hour or two, he turned in. He was more tired that he had realized and quickly fell asleep.

Toward dawn, Bolejack suddenly awoke. Had he heard something, or had he just been dreaming? He lay in the dull gray pre-morning light with his eyes open as he listened. There it was again. The sun was now struggling to claw its way through a low bank of clouds. Bolejack's hand inched toward his Colt tucked under his saddle. He jerked up, gun in hand, as something dark and heavy threw itself upon him. A knife blade flickered in the light of the dim morning as Bolejack's gun exploded. Something large and smelly landed on top of him. He pushed it away as someone about twenty feet away screamed, "Bolejack!"

Again, Bolejack's Colt barked in the thin morning air as his horse whinnied wildly nearby. A hot stinging sensation burned his left arm as he jerked to one side and fired again and again at the advancing shadow. A scream slashed the air as the shadow fell while wildly firing off another round.

Then there was quiet. But the mass next to Bolejack suddenly grunted and sat up. Again, an arm with a knife raised into the air and Bolejack fired again. There was another groan as the dark thing fell back, silent forever.

Bolejack sat there a moment, waiting for another attack, but there was nothing. Mechanically, he reached for his holster hung on the saddle horn and pulled it toward him. He reloaded.

Unsteadily rising to his feet, he walked over to a mound of brush he had reluctantly prepared for a fire the night before. He lit it and then stared at the two dead strangers who had tried to kill him. He didn't know their names, but their faces were vaguely familiar. He thought they were probably two of Black's men. He let the fire blaze. He didn't care now if they could see it or not. Let them come.

He looked nervously across the sandy basin. There would be more of them. He'd have to get moving. But not before coffee. Let'em come, Bolejack thought to himself. Let'em come.

Chapter 24

"So just what are we? A posse, a lynch mob or something else?" Isac Karp said as he sat glumly around the leaping campfire.

"We're anything we want to be," Black mumbled back. "Maybe we're vigilantes of a sort."

Karp's face twisted up in disgust. "I'm regretting I came along already."

"You can do that," Black said, "but you're helping to save yourself as much as me."

Chick slowly shook his head. He wished he hadn't come along, too. It had been two days of hard riding with nothing much to show for it. They had picked up Bolejack's trail and the trail of the two Black Cross men that were following him, but that was it. He wished he had been told to stay at the ranch with Rose like Josh Barnes had. But here he was. How many men did it take to kill this Bolejack anyway?

"We better be turning in," Karp stoically said.

"Go on," Black said, "I'm not ready yet."

Most of the other men were already snoring as Karp slowly prepared his spot on the sandy soil. As he pulled the coarse red and black horse blanket over him and rested his head on the hard surface of his saddle, he gazed out once more at the solitary figure of Clay Black hunched over the dying fire. Sometimes he imagined what if King Westrum hadn't disappeared and had kept his part of the bargain. But he had, and for years his ghost had haunted both him and Black. If things had only happened differently….

"They're dead, I tell you! They're dead! All three of them!" the agitated cowboy was screaming as he did some sort of weird jig as Karp bolted upright.

Black was standing strangely immobile as the hysterical man continued his bizarre marionette-like prancing.

"Calm down, man!" Black finally blurted from his stupor. "Who's dead?"

"Lucas Frye, Pete Ward and Ike Jones—all murdered in their sleep! And me—I was sleeping right next to them!"

"What the hell, Clay!?" Karp found himself hissing as he struggled to his feet. "Was it Bolejack?"

Chick Swickard had come running and now stood beside his boss. "Anybody else?"

"Just those three."

"But how?"

A fire, like the flame from a struck flint sprang to Black's eyes. "Go bury them."

"Now?"

"Now."

Isac Karp walked slowly toward Black. "How on earth could Bolejack--?"

Suddenly a weariness and a deep fear came to Black's eyes. "I don't think it was him."

"You mean—" Karp began. "But that couldn't be—it's been years since…."

"Aw, hell," Chick mumbled as he walked away. "Get the shovels, boys."

Wooly James watched from the distance as Bolejack broke camp, then slowly lead his horse up the grade. He hadn't slept much that night, and fatigue was beginning to catch up with him. He was an old man now, but sometimes he forgot. He had to slow down.

As he rode up onto the ridge where Bolejack had camped, the first thing he noticed were the two freshly dug graves. There was no need to dig these up. Who knew who they were or even cared. They were either Black's or Karp's men. He had been trailing them and another set of tracks for as long as he had trailed Bolejack. But he was surprised they had caught up with the man before he had. But it didn't matter, he thought to himself, he had been quite busy that night himself.

Wooly was tempted to stop now, make camp, cook breakfast and sleep. But it was a fresh day, and he knew that Black, Karp and their men would soon be behind them. "Guess I'll just wait and sleep tonight," Wooly said to no one. *'Maybe I am going senile,'* he thought to himself—*'talking to myself.'*

Wooly sat there a few more minutes. He glanced back down the basin and saw nothing. Then he looked south and made out the moving dot that was Bolejack. "Well, hell," Wooly said aloud. "At least when I talk to myself, I know I'll have an intelligent conversation."

Chapter 25

It was nearing the end of another long and monotonous day. Wooly had pushed his horse hard to catch up with Bolejack. He was tired of the chase, the secrets, the bloodshed.

Bolejack had stopped at a small river to water his horse. He sat atop it now rolling a cigarette when Wooly noisily rode up from behind. In an instant Bolejack had dropped his makings and twisted around in his saddle, gun drawn.

"It's just me," Wooly shouted as he raised his empty hands. "Just me."

Bolejack sheathed his weapon and looked curiously at the old man. *'Now I can tell him the truth,'* Wooly thought to himself as he dropped his hands and smiled.

But then, seemingly out of nowhere, a shot split the thin evening air. Bolejack jerked erect as he pivoted his head around. Wooly, about to say something, only looked surprised as he slumped to his right and fell to the ground.

Quickly, Bolejack was off his horse and behind a small pile of rocks at water's edge. He cocked his gun, ready to fire. Nothing. He looked at the unmoving thing that had once been Wooly James. Moments passed. Then there was a soft rustling in some brush downstream.

Bolejack fired at it. There was silence and then the faint clop of horse hooves.

Whoever had shot Wooly was now gone. Bolejack scanned the scattered tree line expecting to see a contingent of Black's men. There was nothing. Besides, no matter where or what Black or Karp were, they were not bushwhackers.

Bolejack buried Wooly where he had fallen. He wondered why he had so suddenly appeared. There were a lot of unanswered questions about Wooly James, questions that now would never be answered. Or would they?

It was nearly dark now so Bolejack made camp by the river. As sleep began to overtake him, he gazed at the rock-covered grave of Wooly. *'Was that even his real name,'* he wondered? Somewhere, a solitary coyote questioned the night.

Chapter 26

Bolejack broke camp before sunrise. He didn't bother with breakfast or coffee. He knew Black and his men were surely gaining on him now. It was still many miles to the Mexican border. And even then, what was to stop Black from following him?

The tenuous combination of Black's and Karp's men was becoming more frayed all the time. Isac Karp was getting more and more restless as well as increasingly bored. He wanted to get back to Maggotwood and his saloon. He was getting too old and fat and soft for the trail. Not that he had ever been much of a cowboy or frontiersman to begin with, even when he was young. In the early days he had helped Black with the ranch and acreage they had so adroitly acquired from Westrum. But Karp had always preferred town to the ranch—gambling to ranch work. When Black had paid him off for his part of the land, Karp had quickly and quite successfully invested in Maggotwood. In fact, he now mostly owned it. Yes, Westrum's land had made both him and Black wealthy. But Westrum had gone sour on the deal. That's when the mysterious murders and other harassment had begun. Now, years later, Bolejack, Westrum's only living heir, had shown up unexpectedly asking questions—just when things had finally settled down. And just as suddenly, the old troubles had once again restarted.

"Get the boys up and ready!" Black blurted out. "We've already wasted most of the morning."

There was much grumbling, especially from Karp's men as they cut their breakfast short and started preparing to saddle up. They didn't like taking orders from Black.

"The hell with Mexico," one of Karp's men said under his breath so only a few of his companions could hear him. "I'm lagging to the rear when we head out— and when I get the chance, I'm heading off back to town. Anyone with me?"

Three others nodded a silent assent. The others within hearing range only slowly shook their heads.

"Now don't you squeal us out," the mastermind of the scheme whispered to the others. "You don't want no lead belly."

The small group of Karp's men finished their preparations and quietly fell in line. The sun was already hot in the cloudless sky as they urged their horses out. As planned, the four men slowly slackened their pace and fell to the end of the rag-tag parade. About a half hour into the ride, the group came to a high ridge and started up it.

"This is our chance," the ringleader announced as the last four men slowed even more. They stopped before topping the ridge, quickly turned their horses and then spurred them away. It was a minute or two before the rest of Black and Karp's men realized what happened.

"Damn it!" Black exploded. Stunned, Karp watched as the four riders grew smaller.

"I'll send some men after them…" Karp offered, bewildered.

But Black just sat there as they perched on top of the ridge. Karp began issuing orders to his remaining men.

"No, let them go," Black finally said. He sighed and turned his horse back toward Mexico. "We still have enough men. He's only one man, ain't he?"

Karp said nothing, but also turned back in the direction of Mexico. He wished he had thought of it himself—he wished he was with his men heading back. Instead, here he was, following a crazy man to Mexico, hell or worse.

Chapter 27

"Howdy Stranger," the soft voice said.

Bolejack awoke from his daydreams with a start. His eyes had become half-closed as the boredom of his long ride had enveloped him. He had been thinking of this childhood and trying to recall the sound of his mother's voice.

"Who?! What?!"

"Take it easy. It's me," Rose Black said as she rode out of a clump of trees. "I've been following you a long time."

Bolejack shook his head, trying to clear it. "What are you doing here?" He finally managed to say.

"I was worried about you—after I heard Dad ride out."

"He doesn't know you're here?"

"Of course not. He would never have approved."

"I'm not sure I do…."

Rose seemed hurt by his remark, but then quickly recovered. "Well," she cooed, "I don't need your approval either."

In truth, Bolejack was secretly pleased to see her again. She had crossed his mind many times on his trek to Mexico. He had even talked himself into believing that he probably would never see her again.

"You ARE pleased to see me, aren't you?"

Bolejack stroked his thick growth of beard. He hadn't bothered lately to shave—or bathe.

"I must look—" he began.

"Like a rugged, handsome man," she said as she held back a smile.

Bolejack blushed, but then became serious. "You've taken quite a chance being out here. It's dangerous."

"So is life," she piped back.

"You didn't happen to run into Wooly James, did you?"

Rose's face lost its flirtatious glow for a moment as she digested what he said.

"No—not him. But I did catch a glimpse of someone following you—someone tall and dark, not at all like Wooly."

"But you didn't know who it was?"

"No. And I know all my father's men by sight."

A troubled look came to Bolejack. "You know about Wooly?"

"No. I didn't even know he was out here."

"He's dead. Probably shot by the man you saw."

Rose was silent. "I'm sorry. I didn't know. I passed my father and his men, but they didn't see me. And I certainly never saw Wooly."

A faraway look came to Bolejack's eyes. "Who was he? Wooly? He always seemed like a mystery."

"You didn't know?"

"Know what?"

"He was Westrum's foreman. That's what my father told me before he rode out. He figured you remembered him when you were a boy."

Bolejack rocked back in his saddle. Wooly? Wooly was Jim? He had never connected the two. He'd never known his last name. Jim James. Wooly was Jim James?

"He never mentioned it to me, but he was trying to tell me something when he was shot."

"That's odd. Dad said that he came to work for Dad after your family died and you disappeared. But I only vaguely remember him as Jim. Then he quit suddenly. I suppose he became the town drunk after that, but I was too young to realize he was the same man that had briefly worked for us. It all seems so sad now."

"Why…?" But Bolejack couldn't finish his sentence. As with so much more about his father, it all just didn't quite add up. There was still something missing.

"My father's not far away," Rose said finally to break the silence.

"I know."

"I've got a camp of sorts close by."

"You're a surprising woman," he said as they headed off.

"He'll kill you."

"I know," Bolejack said, tonelessly.

"That's why I came."

"I know."

Chapter 28

A lone, dark figure stood over the rock-encrusted grave of Wooly James. His head was bowed as thoughts of recent and long-gone days fluttered through his mind.

"I didn't want to do it," the man said aloud. But he had done what he must. There was always the greed. Greed that ate at him even now. He wanted it—he still wanted it all. He had only let Clay Black retain his land because he had no way to reclaim it. He had signed over his land to save his own life. But what Black and Karp didn't know was that he still had the original deeds to the land. But in court he wasn't sure the old deeds would be valid.

Even now he wasn't sure why he signed the deeds Black now held. Was it just to save his own hide? He hated to admit it, but he hadn't cared about his family. It was then and only then that he realized he was an evil man. But receiving money for his land and to save his life wasn't enough. That's when he had begun the raids. But it was still all for him—his greed. It wasn't for any revenge for his family. That was what really made him a bad man. But Black had fought back—in fact, he'd nearly killed him—twice. But Wooly James had been there to save him. And this was how he had repaid him. Death. But Jim, or Wooly, as he later called himself, had grown apart from him—he had felt it. Then, when his only heir, his lost son, had suddenly reappeared, Wooly had turned away from him.

I'm just an old man now, King Westrum mumbled to himself. But still the greed held him. That's why he had raided Black's ranch, and why he felt no fatherly love of his only surviving son—a man who had shunned his name and was only known as Bolejack. Yes, somehow his son had survived and made his way in life without him or his money. Hell, he didn't even want to claim his name, and now, he'd never claim a foot of his land either!

"Bolejack!" Westrum screamed aloud as he turned away from Wooly's grave. "What kind of name is that?!"

Yes, he'd made his secret deal with Karp, too. But Karp was only his employee. It was really Westrum that owned Maggotwood and the surrounding area including the Black Cross ranch. In fact, he'd even bought off some of Karp's own men to help raid Black's ranch and shoot his men. Yes, he had invested wisely over the years, but he still wanted back everything that was once his. Bolejack? Even in death his so-called son would be denied this rightful inheritance. But he was no son of his—not really. That life, that part of him was dead years ago.

As he rode away, the trace of a smile on his lips had disappeared. His plan had been working perfectly—until Bolejack showed up. He'd thought he'd just waltz in here, solve the mystery of his birthright, and claim his rights to the wealth of his dead daddy. That was the funny part: his daddy. Bolejack thought he was the son of King Westrum, but he really wasn't. The cruel joke was on him. He was the real bastard, the bastard son of Wooly James. Maybe that was why he hated him, his wife and his dead son. Was even that son really his? But now, even that secret was in its grave.

A strange half-cocked smile returned to Westrum as he rode on. That's why Bolejack would never have the land and wealth of King Westrum. And that's why, in the end, he had to kill Wooly. Wooly was going to tell it all.

"Get up!" Westrum grunted as he spurred his horse. He had planned to stop Bolejack before he crossed into Mexico. But, on second thought, he'd let Black do it instead. Then the real reckoning with Black and Karp would come at last. Two empty graves, he thought to himself, as he rode on. Two empty graves. Black had thought he'd killed him twice already. Maybe he wouldn't live much longer, but it would be longer than Black did. That was how the game worked.

Chapter 29

"I'll have a reputation now," Rose Black said as she leaned over the campfire. "Sleeping out here under the stars with a strange man…."

"Am I that strange?" Bolejack replied. He blinked his sleep-heavy eyes at the rising sun.

"Some might say so."

Bolejack watched Rose as she adjusted the battered blue graniteware coffee pot over the flames. The intoxicating aroma of baking biscuits, bacon and boiling chicory coffee brought him to full wakefulness.

"Does this mean I'm obliged to marry you now?" he teased.

"Only if you want too—it's not like my father is after you with a shotgun—or maybe he is, come to think of it."

"I'm afraid I could be dead before you break the happy news to him."

"You could be," Rose said as her smile faded.

"Who's been raiding your father's ranch and killing his men?" Bolejack suddenly asked as his playful mood vanished.

"We don't know."

"I think your father knows."

Rose didn't say anything as she handed him the tin plate of food. She slowly shook her head. "He doesn't discuss it with me," she said after carefully chewing a half-burnt biscuit.

"And has he discussed why he wants to kill me?"

Rose returned his gaze sadly before she answered. "It's the land," she said, "it's always the land."

"He thinks my claim to it is real then?"

"Yes… that… and the fact you keep asking about King Westrum."

"I had the feeling Wooly was going to tell me something when…."

"When he was shot? Yes, maybe that was part of it but—"

"But what?"

"You don't know for sure, and now you'll never know."

"That's true."

"And now you've got my virtue."

"Now wait a minute. We never—I mean I stayed in my blanket and you stayed in yours."

"But who will believe that?" Rose twittered as she winked at him and gathered up the empty tin plates.

"So, I guess I'll have to marry you then?"

"Well," Rose beamed, "you know that old story about getting the cow's milk free…?"

Bolejack got to his feet quickly and turned away blushing. "What milk?"

"You have heard that one, haven't you?" she coyly asked on the verge of laughter.

"We need to saddle up and get going," he said as he walked toward the horses. *'Damn women…'* But he knew he was fooling no one, not even himself.

Chapter 30

The overly unctuous Isac Karp brushed back the long stringy strands of his greasy red hair after he pulled the floppy hat off his sweaty head. It was going to be another long hot day. He wondered why he'd ever left the cold climate of his childhood state of Minnesota for the dry wasteland of this rattlesnake-infested state. But he already knew the answer: money and opportunity.

The rift between Karp's men and the hands of the Black Cross Ranch had continued to grow. But that was a good thing. He knew the time was drawing nigh for a parting of their ways, and it couldn't come soon enough for him and his men. He had never really cared much for Clay Black from the very beginning. It had always been a partnership of convenience and necessity. What Black had done to Westrum had never sat well with him, but he hadn't tried to stop it, he had just looked on and accepted his portion of the bounty. After all, he did have ethics— just not all that many. And he had had the final laugh at Black's expense and Black didn't even know it. He wondered if Rose knew. Besides, he thought as his mind drifted back to Westrum, they had paid him off—at about a quarter of the land's value and threw in his life to boot. If they had simply killed him, there would have been no trouble now; at least not from him. But still there would have been Bolejack.

It had been the impressive aura and will of Clay Black that has brought the once mighty King Westrum down. It had even surprised him. But the real surprise was when Black discovered that he hadn't really eliminated Westrum at all after he had gone rogue—that he still lived. Yet Black remained the legal owner of the property once claimed by Westrum, and that's the way it would always be.

Karp could see Black getting his horse ready for the day's ride. He wondered what the man would do if he knew the truth about him and his daughter—how even now he lay in wait for Westrum's final order? He'd shoot him, that's what he'd do. That was always the answer for any question Black wanted answered.

They'd lost a man, one of Black's, the day before. His sorrel had stepped into a hole, breaking its leg and throwing the rider. They'd shot the horse. The rider's neck was broken, and he'd died instantly. It could have been the other way around. That's how life goes.

"We'll take it easy today," Black told him when he rode up. "We've been pushing the horses too hard. We'll make camp before sundown—there's no reason to rush now, I suppose."

"No rush," Karp agreed. All the men were tired. They'd seen their numbers diminish by death, desertion and accident. It had become a death march of sorts. All Karp really wanted to do was turn back, but he knew he couldn't do that—not yet—not till his task was finished.

"Make sure your canteens are filled," Black called back, "I'm not sure if we'll come across any more water tomorrow. We're riding into a dry stretch." As usual there was the low rumble of disapproval from the men. They were already on their third set of fresh horses with few prospects for replacements up ahead.

"I feel like I'm back in the damned Cavalry," one of Black's men groused as they all began slowly riding out.

"Yeah," said another, "the Seventh Calvary—and Black's acting like Custer. All we need now are Indians."

Chapter 31

"Who's grave is that?" Chick asked as the jerry-rigged posse stopped.

"We could dig it up and see," one of Karp's men quipped. "It'd make about as much sense as what we're doing now."

"Shut up, Jack!" Chick spat back.

"We ain't digging nobody up," Black said flatly. "I'm sure it's not Bolejack."

"Westrum? Again?" Karp said in a low voice only Black could hear.

"Quiet…" Black muttered under his breath. He sat up straight in the saddle and looked around. "This is as good a place as any to camp—and there's water."

The relieved men began dismounting. All their nerves were on edge. Karp remained on his horse a few moments as he fumed. No man told him to be quiet.

"Are you getting down or not?" Black finally said as Karp continued to sit atop his horse unmoving.

"One day you'll say too much, Black," Karp said as he dismounted at last.

"Yeah? Well maybe I didn't care for some of your wise cracks either, you fat old fool—"

Karp's hand edged toward his pistol. *'No, not now,'* he told himself. *'Not now.'*

Black led his horse away to a scrawny tree and loosely tied it. "Chick!" he shouted. "Get the rope corral up and tend to my horse."

Chick came up meekly and led Black's horse away. He gave a knowing smile to Karp. He had heard.

"We'll push harder tomorrow," Black said, almost to himself. "Go a few miles east—I know a rancher there. We can get fresh horses."

Karp heard him, but didn't answer. He didn't care at all really. He just wanted it done and over. Where was Westrum? Why all this dragging on and on? Could it be that he really was in that grave? No, he told himself—not Westrum, he was too smart for that. Too smart even for Black—only Black didn't know it yet. Black had had his run. King Westrum had only been playing with him. It would already have been all over if it hadn't been for Bolejack riding in and gumming up the works. Yes, they'd see Bolejack dead first, then….

Karp jerked to attention when he heard the first shot. Then came more shots. The horses in the rope corral, reared in fright. Several of the cowboys frantically tried to quiet them.

"What's going on?" Black yelled. He had been dipping his canteen in the water of the small river when the shots were heard. Upstream a tangle of men churned in the rising dust.

"One of Karp's men shot Johnny Redmon!" Chick yelled back. "Shot him dead."

"Tie him up!" Black barked back. "We'll deal with him in the morning."

Another one down, Karp thought to himself. Another one down.

"And no poker games tonight," Black bellowed. "We don't need any more shootings tonight!"

Karp mumbled to himself, "at this rate there won't be any of us left to shoot Bolejack if we do catch up with him."

Chapter 32

"All Mexico is good for is hiding and dying," Rose said suddenly as they were riding. "It's not a place for living—at least not for an American."

"No country for gringos," Bolejack answered as a slight smile crossed his lips. He hadn't smiled for days it seemed like, and even now the remnants of this one quickly disappeared.

"You should go back," Rose said.

"Me? You're the one who should go back. There's nothing for you in Mexico."

"And there's something for you there?"

He scowled as his eyes played over the dry, sparse terrain ahead. "Yes… freedom. Life. What else is there?"

"Your land. Your property. Your legacy. Your respect. Isn't that worth fighting for?"

He didn't answer. He raised his hand and pointed to some buildings up ahead. It looked like a modest adobe ranch. "Maybe they've got a horse they'd sell," he said.

"Then you're going on to Mexico…?"

"I'm going on even if I have to walk."

Rose was silent and remained so as they rode on. A weathered sign simply stated: McCrone Ranch. As they neared a large barn three men appeared and stood watching them.

"Howdy," Bolejack said as he raised his hand in greeting.

"How do," the bigger of the men answered, he lowered the shotgun in his left hand. "Something we can do for you?"

"We're just riding through on the way to Mexico and wondered if you might have a good horse or two for sell or trade. Ours are getting frazzled as you can tell."

"We can probably work a deal," the big man said as he eyed Rose. "I'm the owner here. John McCrone. Step on down and we'll work something out."

A few minutes later they were back on the trail with fresh horses. Suddenly Rose reined her horse and stopped. "This is crazy. I'm going back," she said as her face clouded.

Bolejack nodded. He had brought his horse to a stop and looked back.

Rose slowly turned her horse around. "I'll be waiting," she said. Then she shook her reins and started back.

Bolejack just sat there as he watched her disappear. He knew she was right. But when do you give up the dream? Maybe he'd already given it up. Maybe that's why he was running. Was he a coward running for his life, or was he just running away from himself? No. That wasn't him. He could never be that man. He was someone else.

But they were coming. As slow and deliberate as death. He shook his head and sighed. At last, he turned his horse back toward Mexico and started on once again. But why? His future was riding back to Maggotwood. Yet, still he rode on, on to Mexico and oblivion. It was then, and only then, that he knew what he must do. Sometimes a man had to die before he could live.

Chapter 33

Tears curled softly down Rose's dusty cheeks as she rode away. She slowed now, hoping that Bolejack would ride frantically in pursuit of her. He didn't. But she had guessed that already. That would not have been like him. She sighed heavily, then rode on at full trot. "She'd tried," she told herself, but it was not to be. She now resigned herself to never seeing him again, or worse, seeing his lifeless body brought back by her father.

"Damn!" she said aloud as she kept riding. This wasn't the way she wanted it to end. Did she love him? She wasn't sure. But now her thoughts turned back to her father and the gang of men that rode with him. She could find them, try to persuade her father to end this nightmare, end this blood sport. "Why was is so necessary to kill Bolejack anyway," she asked herself. "Why?"

But it would do no good, she knew. Men like her father were single-minded in their loves and hates. Death was their only answer. He wouldn't listen to her reason. It was pointless, hopeless.

It was then she saw them. She pulled behind a small clump of trees and rocks. She didn't want them to see her—not yet. There were fewer of them now, she noticed. She wondered at that. For a moment she fought back the impulse of galloping into the clearing waving her hands and shouting. No, she couldn't do that. She would not do that. There would be too many questions—her father would be furious at her foolishness. No, she would wait—wait for them to pass, and then she would ride on alone back to the Black Cross Ranch. And she would wish and hope like the fool she was.

King Westrum watched the passing of Black and Karp's men, too. Then he watched Rose ride on after they had passed. *'Silly girl,'* he thought to himself. *'Silly lovestruck girl.'* Despite himself, he almost felt sorry for her. Almost. It would have been easy to follow her, end her dreams with a bullet or a knife in the night, but he had no deep hatred for her like he had for her father. He had other destinies to end. Sometimes, late at night he wondered how his soul had become so black, so evil. He had paid for his very breath back then when he had sold his land and soul for his life, but not for the lives of his wife and his sons. He could have saved them, too, but he hadn't—he had wanted it all. But not them. They would have held him back. That was the blackness in him. He hadn't wanted to save them! And out of guilt he had even faked his own death.

But mere living and a solitary life on a dirt crop little ranch near Tombstone hadn't been enough. Not for the once mighty King Westrum. It was then that he had struck back. But Clay Black was soon tired of his games and the farce of his death. That's when they had really tried to kill him. It was only Wooly James that had saved him—helped him fake a second death and a second grave. That's when his raids on Black's ranch had become really serious and deadly. Evil attacked evil. Then Bolejack came along. No one had counted on that. They had thought he was long dead. Now they wanted him dead—all of them. He had dug up the old moldering bones, reopened the old wounds just when he, King Westrum would have at last staged his final triumphant return.

'Funny,' he thought to himself, *'how even blood cannot overcome the dark recesses of a man's heart, the greed that drives a man to kill all and everything he once loved.'*

Chapter 34

"I don't trust Karp," Clay Black said as he lowered his voice.

"Did you ever?" Chick answered.

Black glanced back at Karp and his men before he replied. "Once, a little, when we first took over Westrum's holdings—then he seemed to change a few years later."

Chick spat out a greasy wad of chewing tobacco. "I always wondered if him and Westrum came to some kind of understanding after we thought we'd killed him on his Tombstone ranch."

"That's when the bad raids began," Black murmured. "You better keep an eye on Karp and his boys."

"I already have been."

It was drawing close to the end of yet another day. That morning they had stopped at John McCrone's ranch and gotten fresh horses. John had mentioned a stranger stopping and getting horses, too. The description sounded like Bolejack, but it was the woman with him that had surprised Black. He didn't know quite what to make of that. If he hadn't known better—but who was the girl? And why would she be riding with Bolejack?

When they followed the trail out of McCrone's ranch they noticed that the two horses had stopped and then one had doubled back. Doubled back—it made no sense, and then one had continued riding on toward Mexico. That had to be Bolejack.

"I don't know, Clay," Chick began, "you're the boss and all, but is following Bolejack clear to Mexico and beyond to kill him all that important? He knows we ain't giving him Westrum's land back and what can he prove or do?"

"He's got the deeds for one thing. And he is Westrum's kid." Black had been having his own doubts lately. But still there burned something in his big frame that wouldn't allow him to turn back, something that had made him almost insanely keep going on in a blind fury of hate.

"We can't let the seed of this Westrum thing live—we need to kill it." Black said.

"We need to finally kill Westrum is what we need to do," Chick said bitterly. "That's what will kill this thing. Then Bolejack won't matter."

"Yes," Black conceded, "yes, we do. We need to burn the tree and the seed will wither and die."

Black motioned for them to proceed. The prospect of Mexico loomed before them like some vague bogeyman. But it was only imaginary. Mexico or America—they were on a mission to kill. Bolejack, Westrum or both—it didn't matter. Mexico or America. There were no borders when it came to death.

Chapter 35

Bolejack could sense for some time that someone was following him other than Black and Karp's men. It could only be whoever killed Wooly. That was the conclusion that made sense.

The Mexico border was now only a few hours away. What then? He doubted it would stop those that wanted him dead. So, what was the point of crossing the border?

The problem had been heavily on his mind since Rose Black had headed back. In Bolejack's mind there were only two answers: turn around and seek out Black's men or find a good vantage point and take a final stand. Either one offered little other than a quick death. But keeping on as he had been, and scampering off into Mexico like a frightened jack rabbit only offered a slower death—a death of both the body and the soul.

Bolejack turned his thoughts slowly over in his mind. He knew there could only be one final answer. *'To hell with it,'* he told himself. He had decided what he was going to do.

"Get down off your horse!" Vonnie Lynch said as he aimed his scarred Colt at Bolejack's heart. The man had appeared out of thin air it seemed. "I could kill you now like Black told me, but I don't do business like that. You know who I am, don't you?"

Bolejack recognized him from the weather-beaten posters tacked on trees and fenceposts all over the state. "Yeah, I've seen your ugly mug before on dodgers. You're Lynch. Vonnie Lynch."

The wiry but tall man smiled. "That's right."

"They say you're fast. Damn fast."

"That's right. Now get off that horse. I won't ask you again."

Slowly, Bolejack got off and stood there silently. He'd heard of Lynch's reputation. Supposedly, he'd killed fifteen men—all in fair fights. He was fast, most likely faster than him. But he had an ego. He was no back shooter. He played by the rules.

"Now move on out a little more," Vonnie said smugly. "I wouldn't want your horse to take a bullet." Lynch knew he could outdraw this man. It would be another notch and a couple of hundred dollars from Black. He had this.

But then Bolejack did something Lynch hadn't expected. He broke the rules. He threw himself forward into the dirt as his arm whipped up with his Colt. Shots tore the air as dust and gun smoke obscured the scene. Bolejack lay motionless, his face in the dirt. Vonnie Lynch proudly stood there, a puzzled look on his face. So, this was how it felt, he said to himself. The gun dropped from his hand and he fell back slowly as if in slow motion. A new continent of blood formed on his chest. He was dead.

Bolejack pulled himself up and began dusting himself off. His hat lay a few feet away with a bullet hole in its crown. Funny, he told himself, how the fast ones get rattled and shoot off mark.

Many miles to the north, Rose Black had made her meager camp. Her supplies were running low and she longed for the comfort and safety of her bed back at the Black Cross Ranch. She realized now that she had been foolish to follow Bolejack, but even so she didn't regret it. Her only regret now was turning back and leaving him.

Tears began running down her cheeks. No. This couldn't be. She hardly knew the man. She couldn't have… but she had, she now realized. Is this how it feels?

She wasn't sure she liked this thing that people so flippantly called love. She had never guessed it would hurt like this. Naively, she had imagined it to be one long storybook tale of sunny days and romantic nights. It was nothing like that. It now sat churning in the pit of her stomach. Love? Ha! She wondered why people even bothered. But deep down she knew the answer to her own question.

'I've got to go back to him!' she found herself screaming in her head. *'I've got to go back!'* How could

she let her father kill the man she loved? *She* had to stop him. Somehow, she had to stop him.

The campfire was burning low when she finally drifted off to sleep. But the next days journey back was clear in her mind. She had never been more certain of anything in her short life. Maybe she was crazy she told herself as sleep enveloped her. Maybe love was just another form of insanity.

Chapter 36

"I say we give up this crazy jackalope chase and head back!" Isac Karp said. He had spit out the words like bits of rotten stew meat. The men had wearily been breaking camp, their bellies only half full due to a sparse serving of salt pork and yesterday's reheated biscuits.

The men stopped their half-hearted preparations and stood silent as all eyes turned in the direction of Black and Karp. It seemed like things had finally come to a head.

"I knew you were always short on guts," Black shot back. Chick Swickart edged forward nervously behind him.

Karp drew himself up to his full five foot seven inches and looked at Black. Tiny bits of spittle glistened around his plump lips. He placed his hands on the dusty lapels of his black suit and gave a possum-like grin. "As I recall, the last man you accused of lacking guts was King Westrum. How did that turn out for you?"

Black's face darkened as he regarded the fat man's strange smirk. He had never really liked Karp and had only played along with him to strengthen their control of the territory. It was obvious now that they were at the end of their long and tenuous union.

"So that's it?" Black finally said at the end of what seemed to be a long and painful silence. "Do you and your boys just turn around now with your little tails between your legs and forget about Bolejack?"

"He still doesn't know the whole truth, does he?" Karp taunted, "or does he? Even if he did, so what?"

"So what?! So what?! He could ruin us all, that's so what!"

Inexplicably, Karp laughed. "The great Clayton Black!" Karp mocked. "A king in his own mind! But you were nothing—nothing without me! The first time Westrum raided your ranch you ran to me! You'd seen a ghost you said! The ghost of King Westrum, the man you thought you'd killed. Ha! You never had any guts or brains—it was me—and the very live ghost of Westrum!"

"You lie!" Black screamed as he cleared leather. The shot jerked everyone to attention as Karp fumbled inside his jacket. He whipped out a derringer and then, just as suddenly dropped it as his vest turned crimson.

Shots rang loudly from every direction. Karp's men had been caught flat-footed. Chick stepped in front of Black as the shell of what had been Isac Karp crumbled before them. Chick and Black's guns flared in the early morning light as Karp's men staggered back with their guns blazing.

Suddenly Chick stopped in mid-motion as a lead slug tore through his forehead and exited from the back of his head. But still he stood for a few seconds as his useless gun hand tried to fire again and again. But it was no good. He slumped forward as Black seemed to lose his footing and trip over a rock.

Then, just as suddenly, the shooting stopped. A haze of smoke seemed to shroud the few remaining figures still standing. Like some primordial thing, Black rose amid the clearing gun smoke and looked at the remaining four men, his men. One clutched his arm, another limped forward. Only Black and two others were unscathed. Karp and his men lay dead or dying.

One of Black's men began to speak: "Are we gonna…?"

"No!" Black said mechanically. "Let'em lie. We don't have time for the dead."

And so it was that the last four men and Black that saddled up and rode out. They were nearing Mexico, but more importantly, they were closing in on Bolejack.

Bolejack, Black thought to himself. Bolejack. He had become an obsession. How could that be? He had had him right in the palm of his hand and had let him get away. How could that be?

The five men rode slowly off. They didn't know what the day or the night would bring. As they diminished from sight, a solitary rider watched. "Hell," King Westrum said to himself, he should have known that Karp couldn't get the job done. Now it was up to him— but it had always been up to him. After all, he was king.

Chapter 37

Rose had heard the shooting. At first, she wasn't sure from which direction it had come. Her father had taught her the rudiments of tracking when she was only a child. She had never been good at it, but she could get by. She searched the parched landscape, but seemed to have lost their trail. Instinctively, she had turned her ear to the south when the shots had rung out. It only made sense that the shooting was ahead of her toward Mexico. She reined her horse on at a slow pace. If only she could find their trail to make sure.

It was the next morning when she came upon the random hieroglyphics of Black's and Karp's men again. Slowly, but methodically she rode on. If she found them, she would also find Bolejack. It was as simple as that.

Toward mid-day she noticed something dark circling in the sky ahead of her. A sudden feeling of dread came upon her. Vultures.

"Oh God, oh God," she found herself muttering under her breath as she spurred her horse forward at a quicker pace. *'Was she too late? Was it all over?'*

Then she saw it. Vultures were hunched over dark masses dotting the land ahead of her. More vultures swooped down and dove into the mayhem. A sickness crept over her as she stopped her horse and watched. Her stomach roiled and for an instant she had the urge to throw up. But she didn't. She wiped her sweaty forehead. Bodies. Dead bodies.

Overcoming the rising tide of nausea, Rose slid clumsily off her horse and ran up to the first body as the huge birds scattered. She grabbed a rifle from the ground and began shooting wildly into the air.

"Get away! Get away!" she screamed hysterically as she ran around in a circle firing into the sky.

Squawking and hissing, the ugly turkey buzzards rose in mass and returned to the fetid air. And like her, they aimlessly circled.

Rose looked on in horror at the rotting and mutilated bodies of Chick Swickard, Isac Karp and the other men. Clay Black was not among the dead.

"Oh God! Dad!" she yelled as she threw down the empty rifle. She stood there then, mute, sickened, but somehow strangely fascinated by the once living things that were splayed before her in the reddened sand.

Her bulging, horrified eyes took at the grotesque scene as flies went madly about their work, and several vultures gathered their courage and dove to earth like dark fallen angels.

"Father…" she whispered to herself. Only now it seemed, did she admit the truth of her real father, Isac Karp. Clay Black had killed him. The man who pretended to be her father had killed him. But now she was done with the charade of shame and convenience. No longer would she bear the name of Black.

Her eyes fell upon the remains on a dead horse. A buzzard perched atop it. She noticed that a short shovel was tied to the saddle. She picked up the empty rifle again and threw it at the winged demon.

"I'll only bury you," she heard herself say, "only you and my name."

Chapter 38

Bolejack had pushed his horse hard once he had made up his mind. He would face his fate, no matter what it was. Up ahead he could see the dust of riders headed his way. It had to be Black, Karp and their men. He had come across no other riders in his journey toward Mexico.

He stopped now to let his horse rest as he built a smoke. They would soon be upon him. Carefully, he eyed the surrounding landscape. It was sparse, dry and bleak. There was no good place for an ambush here, but that was fine. He preferred to meet his pursuers out in the open, face to face. There would be no more running or hiding in an outhouse. At last he was going to face his childish fears.

He had finished a second cigarette by the time Black and the others came into sight. But there was something wrong. He only saw five men. How could that be? Black wasn't hard to pick out, but there was no sign of Karp or Chick. It was just Black and four of his ranch hands.

The men halted when they recognized the lone figure of Bolejack. It seemed to stun them. They hadn't expected to come upon him just calmly sitting there in the open.

"Bolejack?!" Black boomed. "Is that you?" But he already knew the answer.

"Who else?"

"Then you're a fool! A dead fool!"

Bolejack didn't answer. Something moving had caught the corner of his eye to the far right of Black and his men. A lone rider. Then another movement made him turn his head slightly to the left. It was a trap. How many of Black's men were scattered around to kill him?

Black had also seen the riders to his left and right. "They're not with me—if that's what you're thinking," he shouted.

"Shut up Black!" the voice to his left yelled.

Even from that distance, Bolejack could see the color drain from Black's face. "Westrum?" he screamed, but even as his mouth formed the word, Westrum's gun appeared out of nowhere and Black spun crookedly out of his saddle in a spewing mist of red.

"No!" Bolejack shouted, but even as he spoke his gun game out and he began firing. A crackling of explosions and a veil of smoke filled the air as the last of Black's men began firing at any and everything. Westrum's horse reared and threw him backwards. Bolejack had emptied his pistol and now grabbed for the rifle in the scabbard near his saddle. He pounded three shots into the mass of Black's men before something crashed into his shoulder and blew him off his horse.

There was a lull in the shooting as two of Black's remaining men swayed on their horses in the cloud of smoke like drunkards. To Bolejack's right, the final lone rider leveled a rifle and shot the men off their horses.

Bolejack staggered to his feet trying to level his rifle and fire at the remaining rider. "Who…?" he began to say but stopped and slowly lowered his gun. "Rose….?"

Rose slid off her horse and ran to Bolejack. "You're hurt!"

"Rose—I…."

"Sit down, you're bleeding."

Bolejack fell clumsily back into the dirt, but just as suddenly jerked himself back up on his feet. "That other rider—that was Westrum?"

Rose was holding him, propping him up, but he gently pushed her away. He had to see—see for himself.

King Westrum's dead horse had fallen on him, pinning him beneath. As Bolejack and Rose came upon him his eyes fluttered open. He forced a weak smile. "Guess I'm not the king anymore," he whispered, "long live the king."

Bolejack stood above him not knowing what to do or say. "Father?" he said at last.

"I wasn't much of one," Westrum answered. "Wooly…" but the light was beginning to dim in his eyes. Blood soaked the sand beneath him. "The deed. The real deed—in my saddlebag. It's yours. It's all yours."

"Why?" was the only word that came from Bolejack's mouth.

"Sometimes a man… wants too much… but he really has nothing—just lies and a heart turned to stone. I would have killed you just like I let your mother and brother be killed. My soul was empty. Nothing, it's just all nothing."

Bolejack stood alone now as Rose left his side to stand over the body of the man who was never her father. *'Had he known all along?'* she wondered? But now it didn't matter.

"Nothing—" Bolejack repeated as he watched the man, he had never really known fade away. But he felt no remorse, no sadness, nothing. There were no tears. Not now or ever. Perhaps his father had left him another legacy other than the land after all—a hardened heart. He looked up toward heaven, then slowly sunk to his knees, weak from a loss of blood—his blood and the blood of his heritage.

Far away, somewhere in Mexico or perhaps in Arizona, a church bell could barely be heard. Bolejack stood back up as Rose helped him. Yes, he could hear it—they both could hear it. It tolled not once, not twice, but three times. The third time was the charm.